RAVEN RAIN

DAVID STEVER
Cinder Path Press, LLC

RAVEN RAIN

Cinder Path Press, LLC
5319 Tarkington Pl.
Columbia, MD 21044

www.davidstever.com

Cover Design: Brandi Doane McCann/ebook-coverdesigns.com

Cover Photograph: Inga Ivanova/Bigstock

ISBN: 978-09983371-4-2 (paperback)
ISBN: 978-09983371-5-9 (ebook)

Printed in the United States of America

To my children,
Brian, Kevin, and Cassidy
With Love

Prologue

The bullet slammed into the wall behind me, missing my head by a fraction of an inch. It came so close the air brushed my face as it shot past. I crouched behind the wooden front counter in the lobby of the Hotel Atlantic, an old boutique hotel, once the art deco showplace of Port City's Old Town section, but now a foul, dilapidated crack house of crime and iniquity. It was one of those places where you could check in but never check out. The dirtbag who took a shot at me, one Enrique Mendoza, was not too happy I invaded his place of business. But I was hell-bent on ridding the world of his venom and returned fire as he scampered up the once ornate staircase, taking out a decent chunk of his right knee. He screamed but kept moving and disappeared on the second floor.

I clicked the mic on my radio. "Mendoza headed to the second floor. I am in pursuit."

"Delarosa, stay put. Wait for backup," came through my earpiece.

"Copy that." *No way*.

I took the stairs two at a time and stopped at the top. The elevator and stairway were to my left, a long hallway to my right. He was trapped.

"Mendoza," I shouted. "Nowhere to go. Don't make this difficult."

The hallway offered no place to take cover. I went prone and snugged against the wall and waited. It didn't take long. Even in the dim light, I could see a trail of blood leading to the third door on the left. Too much blood for him to stay in there much longer. He'd either come out and face my handsome mug or go through the window and fall thirty feet.

The door opened. "I want a deal."

"No chance."

He shuffled into the hall holding a girl in front of him. A hostage. She was a kid, a teenager—couldn't be more than sixteen. Skinny, with long, dark hair, and naked except for her underpants. He had an arm around her waist and held a gun to her head. "I want the DA, or I kill her right here." She struggled but he gripped her tight and pressed the gun hard against her temple.

Tears rolled down her cheeks. "Let me go. Please," she begged through sobs.

"Let her go, Mendoza." Blood soaked his pant leg from his knee to his shoe. "Don't be stupid. You'll bleed out before the DA shows up. Drop the gun and I'll guarantee an ambulance here in a minute."

"No way. Get the DA. I have information. Solid information. Names, sources. He'll want to talk to me."

"You'll never make it. That right knee must be really painful. I'm surprised you can stand." I stared at her while I talked, and prayed she tuned in.

"You have ten seconds to make the call."

I pressed my mic. "It's Delarosa. We're in a bit of a negotiation. He wants the DA. I'll try to keep him alive until he gets here."

"Delarosa. What? What are you doing—"

I cut off my radio—and my captain. "You heard me call. Let her go and we'll find something to wrap around your leg. Hurts like hell, doesn't it?" I kept my eyes riveted on hers. *C'mon, baby.* "You need to get off the leg. That right knee. You're bleeding out."

She looked down and then back to me. I gave her a slight nod. I hoped we were on the same wavelength. And we were.

In one swift motion, she brought her right leg up high, then slammed her foot back into his knee. He screamed and fell, landing hard on his back. She darted into the room, and I emptied my magazine into his body.

I pressed my mic. "Don't interrupt the DA's golf game. Situation contained. Mendoza is down. Need the meat wagon. And Child Services, too."

I got to my feet and checked Mendoza for a pulse. Gee, too late. I stuck his gun in my pocket and went into the room.

She wasn't there. "Hey, where are you? You did great. You read my mind." I clicked on the bathroom light and roaches scattered to the corners. No girl. Black grime lined the toilet bowl and the sink. I guess housekeeping skipped this room. A full-size bed with a sagging mattress, threadbare sheets, and an old army blanket bunched up in a ball was in the center of the room. A small TV sat on a dresser with a microwave oven, a box of cereal, and two boxes of microwave popcorn. A trash can in the corner overflowed with fast-food bags and soda cans. More stains than I could count dotted the worn carpet. *Was she living here in this squalor? Or working? Or both?*

I opened the closet door. She was on the floor, hugging her knees to her chest. I reached out. "C'mon. Let's get you out of here. I know you were scared, but it's over." She didn't move. The only other thing in the closet besides the girl was a ratty, gray, zip-up hoodie on a hanger. "Why don't you get dressed?" She shook her head. "You can't stay here." She would not budge. "What's your name?" Nothing.

"Do you have clothes?" I asked.

The dresser had two drawers. I opened the top one and found a T-shirt, a pair of jean shorts, and two pair of underwear. And a box of condoms. "Is this all your clothes?" The bottom drawer was full of junk. Papers, a man's shoe, pens, pencils, two bottles of whiskey, a carton of cigarettes, and a lot of trash.

"Tell me your name. Mine is Johnny. I'm with the police and I want to help you. Come on out. You'll be safe now." I took the few pieces of clothes from the drawer and placed them on the bed, then went back to the closet and offered a hand. "C'mon." She shook her head. "You can't stay here. Child Services is on their way."

That moved her. "No, no, please. They'll put me in the system. I can't do that." She jumped up and grabbed my arm. "Please don't. I don't want to be in the system. I'm fine on my own."

"You are not fine. You're turning tricks. Are you using?"

"No, no. I swear, man. I don't use."

I held her wrists and scanned her arms. No tracks, which I was glad to see. Her skin was tan; mixed-race, I thought. Had to be starved and malnourished. She was so thin every rib was visible, and her filthy underpants hung off her bony hips. She had long, stringy, tangled, black hair, and she had an odor as bad as the room. She could not have bathed in weeks. But she had these vivid, emerald eyes and I couldn't stop staring. Eyes that belonged on the cover of a fashion magazine, not hidden in the obscenity of a crack-house hotel. I had her put on the T-shirt, shorts, and the hoodie. She wore everything she owned.

The backup units arrived, along with my screaming captain. I explained what went down; he told me what would happen next, scolded me for not waiting for back-up (which I deserved), and said I'd be placed on administrative leave until the investigation was closed.

The girl would not talk, which only made things worse. She could easily back up my story, but only sat and stared at me, hoping, I think, I would come to her rescue. The captain gave up trying to get through to her and said she would have to go with Child Services. As luck, or fortune, or fate, would have it, Child Services was delayed. Crime Scene had finished; it was me and the captain and two other officers waiting for the medical examiner.

I don't know why I did it. Many times, over the course of my career I had pulled kids from dangerous, abusive situations. But there was something about this girl. Don't know what, but I had this overwhelming desire to help. I convinced the captain to allow me to wait with her until Child Services arrived. He agreed, saying it was penance for me, but mostly because he was late for his daughter's high school basketball game.

As soon as he left, we looked at each other—still on the same wavelength. We hurried down the back stairs of the hotel and out to an alley.

"My car is around the corner. I'll take you to my place and you can wash up. I'll make you something to eat. From there, I don't know what."

She nodded. Then, to my surprise, she grabbed my hand as we ran to my car.

She was wide-eyed as we entered my half-empty apartment. I had moved in three months prior after my wife, Kelly, and I separated. I had a bed and dresser, a dinette table, a sofa, and a TV. But to her it must have seemed like a five-star resort. I gave her a towel, wash cloth, soap, shampoo, and turned the shower on for her. A half-hour later, she emerged with the towel wrapped around her, transformed into a different person. She was tall, lanky, with long, black hair, full lips, and those vivid emerald eyes. Her skin was a beautiful shade of light brown, but even more so, she was now a fresh-faced teenager who should be in high school, where the most suffering she should endure was the awkward angst of her teen years.

She stood in front of me as if preparing to make an announcement, which she did.

"Thank you for killing him," she said, without any hint of emotion. Then she clicked on the TV and plopped down on the sofa.

"Was he your pimp?"

She only shrugged so I didn't push it. I gave her a sweatshirt and a pair of running shorts. But the shorts were too big, so she wore the sweatshirt like a dress. I fixed her a turkey sandwich and some macaroni and cheese, the only food I had in the apartment. She devoured it, asked for seconds. Ten minutes later, she was vomiting into the toilet while I held back her hair. "I guess we should pace ourselves with the food."

She fell asleep on the sofa, so I threw a blanket over her and tucked a pillow under her head. While she slept, I went to a twenty-four-hour Walmart and bought everything I could think a teenage girl would need. Jeans, shorts, T-shirts, sweats, pajamas, underwear, shoes, a hairbrush, toiletries, a backpack, and even a portable radio with headphones. I had no idea what size she wore, so I bought everything in three different sizes and figured I'd take back what didn't fit. I even bought a small stuffed animal, a pink bunny.

The next morning, she was over the moon with the new clothes. She would go in the bedroom, put on an outfit, prance down the hallway to the front room as if it were a fashion runway, spin around, and wait for my applause. Then do it again with a different outfit. She did give me a smile and a hug, and that made it all worth it. The headphones became a permanent part of her head as she went from station to station on the radio.

She still would not talk. I would ask her name, where she grew up, what she liked to do; did she run away, did she have any friends? Nothing. She would only stare at me, eat, watch television, and listen to her radio. She took over the front room and had her clothes in neat piles on the floor. The second night, she took another long shower and fell asleep on the sofa hugging the pink bunny.

I stood and watched her as she slept and wondered whether she suffered from some type of traumatic stress disorder. It was inevitable she would need Child Services, mental health services—Mendoza destroyed her—and foster care, but before that, she needed a thorough examination by a doctor. I knew she could not stay with me forever, but I thought if I could make her comfortable and earn her trust, maybe she would open up and allow me to arrange for the help she needed. I also wanted to find out where she was from. Someone, somewhere, must miss her.

On the third day, I brought home a pizza, which we ate together at the table. After dinner, I promised we would go out for ice cream, but I wanted to shower first. I no sooner got shampoo on my head when the shower door slid open. She stood there, naked. I looked into those large eyes. "This is not about that," I said. She stepped in and reached up to kiss me, but I stopped her. Her eyes went to the floor, and she turned and walked out.

I hurried and toweled off, rehearsed what I needed to express to her: A real man would not hurt or abuse her, and there were good people in the world who would help her. And someday she would meet someone who would love her and treat her with respect. I finished dressing, and when I got out to the living room—she was gone. Her clothes, backpack, radio, and her pink bunny were gone. I found a note on the kitchen table.

Johnny. Thank you. I love you.

I never saw her after that. I kept a constant lookout for her as I went about my days. Each week, I checked with social services, foster care agencies, homeless shelters, rescue missions, church programs, but I never found her. I quit after a few months, but I never stopped thinking about her and where she might be, what she was doing, who she was with—was she safe, or on the street, back at the only life she knew?

I prayed she made her way to a shelter and into foster care and placed in a nice home in the suburbs with a loving family and was going to high school every day and making new friends.

But my jaded years as a cop told me the truth.

The girl with the emerald eyes...I prayed she was alive.

1

Over the course of my twenty-year career in the Port City Police Department, and another six on my own as a private investigator, I found myself in plenty of precarious situations. Dodging bullets, high-speed car chases, breaking through doors not knowing who or what to expect on the other side, working undercover with a constant risk of being exposed, and infiltrating organized crime families with nothing but my wits to protect me. All of that was scary enough, but perched on the top of a twenty-four-foot extension ladder leaned against the side of my beach cottage was my least favorite precarious spot of all. My left hand had a white-knuckle grip on the top rung while I hammered a piece of clapboard siding back in place with my right.

"Hold the ladder." I forced myself to peek down at my assistant Katie, who was charged with the ladder-holding duty. She had one hand on the ladder and was checking her phone with the other.

"I am."

"You're sending a text."

"I'm searching for a song."

"Use two hands."

"Why don't you pay somebody to fix it?"

"No, I'm handy, just not fond of being up this high." The only advantage to the ladder was the gorgeous view of the Crescent Beach shoreline and the surrounding homes. My place was not the biggest, brightest, or the most modern, but it was perfect for me. I drove another nail into the siding and made my way down. "I'm not doing that again."

"What's this?" She held my nail gun in her hand.

"A nail gun and please put it down before you shoot yourself."

"Can I try it?"

"Yes, you can help nail the trim around the windows. Right after beer time."

I went inside the house and pulled two bottles of a local ale from the fridge while she stretched out on a deck chair. I salvaged the beach house from my ex-wife, Kelly. It was all that remained of our marriage, and we hung on to the joint ownership much longer than we intended. She was engaged to an endodontist who was not too keen on her still owning property with me. So when I scored a fat payday some months ago, I offered to buy out her half and she agreed. Over the last six weeks I chipped away at improvements. Repairing the siding and some outside window trim work were the final touches on the fix-up. My plan was to live here as much as I could.

I went out to the deck and to my tall, comely assistant. "You're distracting."

"How so?"

"The bathing suit."

"You've seen a girl in a bikini before."

"Not you, though." She wore a scanty black bikini which worked wonders with her tan skin and long mane of blonde hair.

"You are tanning more than working." I handed her a beer.

"I held the ladder. The deal was I help and suntan at the same time."

A nasty attitude had replaced her usual enthusiastic, cheery nature. "Are you still mad?"

She lifted her sunglasses and shot me a look with her ice-blue, man-killing eyes that almost knocked the bottle from my hand.

"Katie, c'mon."

"I wanted to go. No reason to not take me."

"We talked about this. I'm nervous about using you in the field. I'm not sure you are ready to go back out. It might be too soon."

"Shouldn't I be the one to decide?"

A recent job we worked ended with people being shot and Katie experiencing the trauma of violence up close. She disappeared for three weeks, and Mike and I thought she was long gone. Then one day she showed up at our bar ready to work—her spirit rejuvenated and her enthusiasm renewed.

"How about we decide together? The next client."

"I'm not sitting, doing research. I realize that is part of the work, but I want to be in the field. I need more apprentice field hours. I've racked up plenty of computer hours. I'll never get my license at this rate."

I pulled a chair next to her. "We'll assess the next job and decide what you can do. Okay?"

She peeked at me over her sunglasses and clicked her beer bottle on mine.

"Last night was uneventful, and you can't stay mad at me. What other employer allows you to take a suntan and drink beer in the middle of the day?"

"Not complaining. I just want to advance my career."

"How about we advance to the window and finish so I can paint and be done?"

"Fine."

Her mood lightened when I showed her how to connect the nail gun to the compressor and gave her a quick lesson. There were two windows that faced out to the deck that needed new trim. I held the new boards while she went along with the gun.

"What a turn-on. Gives me a tingle every time I pull the trigger."

I should have snapped her picture. A tall blonde in a black bikini, wearing safety goggles, firing a nail into the woodwork. She could have made the cover of *Home Handyman* magazine.

"Concentrate, please. You'll be the first female PI who can also rehab a house."

"I want to live out here. Me and my friend Mandy for the summer."

"No."

"Why not? It would be cool to stay at the beach."

"Parties. I don't want any parties in my house."

"Johnny, c'mon. We won't party."

"You're twenty-four—you will. Plus, I want to use the house on the weekends if Mike doesn't need help. And you work the weekends anyhow. So, no." We finished the trim on the second window. "You are welcome to use the house any time you are not on the clock."

"Two bedrooms—you have yours and Mandy and I could share one. Although, she does think you're cute. For an old guy."

"Nice try."

Her cell chirped and she answered. "Mike," she mouthed to me. "He's right here...you mean the car dealer? Wow...*Buy your car the Shelton way, at Stan Shelton Chevrolet.*" She sang the jingle. "Sorry." She listened for a second, then said to me, "He says Stan Shelton is in the bar and wants to hire you. Us."

"Oh yeah?"

She went back and forth between me and Mike. "Stan can come back at two." I nodded; she confirmed it and hung up. "Wow, the car dealer. This might be interesting."

"Change your clothes. We'll head back in."

"I am def working this job."

She changed while I gathered up my tools, the nail gun, compressor, and the extra wood, and put everything inside the cottage. I had to admit, Stan Shelton needing a private investigator piqued my curiosity.

We got into my Z4 and she started with the jingle again. "*Buy your car the Shelton way, at Stan Shelton Chevrolet.*"

"You're not going to sing that the entire way back, are you?"

"Kind of catchy—and now stuck in my head."

"By the way, I am not old. Only forty-eight."

"Uh huh."

2

Katie and I parked the car in my garage behind the bar and came in through the kitchen and stood in amazement. Lunch time at McNally's Irish Pub was never too busy. A few regulars made it worth being open, but this day was a definite exception.

"Now there is a hot-looking old guy," Katie said, instinctively fixing her hair.

Stan Shelton held court in the center of the bar, surrounded by star-struck patrons who could not soak up enough of his glory days on the football field—and he did not disappoint. A born storyteller, he went from his three years as the starting quarterback at Central Catholic High School, to taking Notre Dame to two bowl games—winning one on a miracle Hail Mary—to being drafted in the third round by the San Diego Chargers. He was well over six feet, broad shoulders, a million-dollar smile, and a few gray streaks added character to a full head of slicked-back black hair. And unlike most ex-athletes, he managed to keep his muscles from moving south to his waistline.

"My dad would be out of his mind right now," she said. "He was one of his heroes. How do you guys know him?"

"He and Mike played together in high school."

"Cool. Can't wait to find out why he wants to hire us."

"Me either."

She snaked her way through the crowd and took over for my tall, barrel-chested, red-haired Irishman of a partner.

Mike spotted me leaning against my booth in the back and walked over. "The king holding court."

"Still larger than life, isn't he?"

"Right where he belongs. In a bar, talking football to a bunch of fans."

"We need to bring him in every day."

Mike shook his head. "He'll want a commission."

He glad-handed and passed out business cards after every story. "Put you in a sweet ride for a price you'll love. Stop in and see me."

The gag was Stan never sold a car in his life. He was the front man, and everyone bought in. Like many ex-athletes, he came back home and invested some dough into a car dealership. The partners stuck his name on the building and in less than eight years, they had three dealerships in Port City. In reality, he played golf four times a week—Port City in the summer, West Palm Beach in the winter—and showed up at the dealership once a month to film a new TV commercial.

I'm not knocking it.

He broke up the fan-fest after another ten minutes and came back to the booth with his hand extended. "Johnny, handsome as ever, man!" He pumped my hand up and down. "Good to see you. How long's it been?"

"Too long. Sit."

I sat opposite and Mike slid in beside me.

"You are right, too long. I need to do this more often. I love it here. This is what I need to be doing. Run a cool bar, have the games on TV, pour drinks all day. Mike, you got it made. You want a partner? Let me buy in."

Mike jerked a thumb toward me. "He's my partner."

"Johnny? You part owner here?"

"Bought half when the Irishman here needed to pay for his divorce."

"Feel for you, Irish Mike. I went through it with wife number one. She was a sweetheart but couldn't handle all the attention. Women paying attention to me, that is. I had no business getting married. We'd go on the road and the hotel would be filled with football groupie pussy. I lost my mind every away game. Then I would come home and be the perfect husband during the week. Until some reporter in Miami did a story about how I liked to party the night before every game. Ended my marriage. First one, anyhow. In the old days, the press would turn their backs. Except for the one self-righteous prick who was mad he couldn't get laid on his own."

"Didn't he have an unfortunate accident after the story came out?" I asked with a wink.

He shrugged. "I heard he broke his hand in a fall down a flight of steps at his apartment building. Freakish thing."

Mike jumped up. "We need to drink to that. Stan, still Scotch?"

"Damn right."

Mike went to the bar and Stan leaned across the table. "Truth is, I'm no better of a man than I was then. I need your help."

"Whatever I can do."

"Someplace we can talk? Too many people around."

"Sure, my place upstairs, but first we drink."

Mike came back with a Scotch, two bourbons, and Katie.

"Stan, meet Katie Pitts, my research assistant, plus she helps out here."

Stan, taken aback by all that was Katie, grabbed her hand and pulled her beside him in the booth. "Pleasure to meet you. I hope these two are doing right by you. Because if they don't, you can come work for me anytime."

She blushed. "Nice to meet you, too, Mr. Shelton."

"Call me Stan, please."

She slid a sheet of paper and a pen in front of him. "An autograph? For my dad? He's a huge fan."

"Of course, darling."

"Make it out to Richard."

Stan scribbled a sentiment.

"Thank you, I appreciate it."

He put his arm around her and she looked at me. "My pleasure. You ever want the real stories about these two, call me." He flicked a business card from his pocket. "I have all the dirt on their sordid past." He followed with a wink and a squeeze of her shoulder.

He crossed the line faster than a wide receiver on a touchdown run. I knew my Katie and she was about to throw a penalty flag on his forward pass. She slid out from under his arm, got out of the booth, and held up the autograph. "Thank you. My dad will love it." She scurried back to the bar.

"A joke, right? She couldn't possibly work for you guys?" He pointed a finger at us. "Which one of you is the sugar daddy?"

"Neither, Stan the man. All business," Mike said. "We don't have the Shelton charm."

"Hell, if she worked for me, I wouldn't last three days without getting sued for harassment."

"Johnny rescued her from a kidnapping about six months ago and she showed up a few days later, wanting to be a PI. We didn't take her seriously at first, but now, she does a bang-up job. Working on her PI license. Not saying we don't like the eye candy, but she can hold her own. We're proud of her."

"No shit. Impressive. Can't begin to count the number of assistants who quit on me or I had to pay to keep quiet."

"Hey, you're Stan Shelton. A toast," Mike said, and we lifted our glasses. "King of the gridiron, lover of women, friend to all men." We threw back our shots. "As long as they are buying a car."

"The Shelton way."

"C'mon, let's go talk," I said. "Tell me how I can help."

"Let's just say it's fourth and long, and the clock is running out."

3

A bottle of Scotch went with us to my fourth-floor condo. Bourbon was more my drink of choice, but I wanted to indulge my potential client a bit.

Stan took a quick scan around my small one-bedroom place, and settled on the sofa. "This is perfect," he said. "Small place, no giant mortgage...do what you want, when you want. I am envious. Me, I have to be everywhere on a schedule. Need the big house, cars, lifestyle. Not complaining, but every so often I'd give anything for a minute to myself."

"Price of fame, huh?" I fixed us both a drink.

"Careful what you wish for."

"You can't make your own schedule? Build in some time for you and your wife?"

"You would think. The problem is Nikki loves the lifestyle. Plays tennis twice a week, is on the board of the country club, theater tickets, benefits, fundraisers. She wants to make sure we are involved in Port City society. She says we must maintain our status within the community."

"Seems you enjoy it."

"I can turn it on. Play the part when I need to. Not denying the celebrity status does wonders for the ego, but it gets old."

I sat down beside him. "Why are you here?"

"Johnny. I'm embarrassed. I did a stupid thing. In a long line of stupid things, but this one has me worried. I was approached by some people, a woman actually, and I'm scared."

"Start at the top." I poured another finger of Scotch in his glass.

"No secret. When it comes to women, I have no self-control. I did things I am not proud of. My first marriage, for example. I can't help myself." He downed the slug of whiskey. "Ever since high school. Hell, senior year, I even cheated on my prom date while we were at the prom."

"Save that story for another time. What is the stupid thing you did?"

"In my infinite wisdom, I decide fooling around with women I meet is too risky, so I checked out the escort services. Money is no problem. Plus no fuss, no muss. I see this one site online, Fantasy, 'we indulge your every desire.'" He made air quotes. "So, I set up a date. This amazing girl shows up, everything works out, and I think I am a genius."

"Where did you meet her?"

"I own a building downtown. One of those lofts buildings. Retail on the ground floor with apartments and offices above. The new, cool, hip office space the millennials want. Lots of windows and ferns. I kept one office for myself in case I wanted to hold meetings there.

Never did, so when I got the escort service idea, I converted the office into an apartment. The girls met me there and when they laid eyes on the cash I laid down, they were more than happy to spend the evening with old Stan. Plus all my equipment works—no little blue pill for me—so no complaints. They are all smoking hot, too. I don't know where they come from, but when I die, I hope I go there."

"Stay focused."

"A week ago I get a call from a man who says he wants me to be a spokesman for their product and do a series of commercials. I tell him to call my agent, but he says they prefer to meet with me first. I agree, and we schedule a meeting at the North Shore dealership. Two days ago. No guy shows up, but this woman walks in, sits down and tells me she knows all about me hiring call girls and how bad it would be for me if that information was made public."

"Blackmail."

"Yes, and I was livid and ready to throw her out of the office but kept telling myself to stay calm. Says the price tag is one hundred thousand or my business with Fantasy is leaked."

"Extortion. You recognize her?"

"Nope."

"What did she look like?" I took out my pad and began jotting notes. I wrote Fantasy Escorts at the top of the page.

"White chick, long blonde hair, freckles all over her face. Mid-thirties, I guess. Slim, beautiful, dressed in a blue business suit. Acted all tough and confident but she fidgeted with her purse the whole time."

"How did she leave it?"

He took a business card from his pocket. "Handed me this and gave me one week." A phone number was printed on the card which I wrote on my paper. "I was in a panic and then thought about you and Mike."

"Cops?"

"Do you know how long it would take for this to leak out if I went to the cops?"

I nodded. "About two seconds. I'm glad you came here. Go back to the beginning. How many girls did you hire?"

"Four, but the fourth one, Dee Dee, six times now. Incredible, amazing, I can't get enough. Not just sex either. A woman never affected me this way."

"Feelings for her?"

He nodded. "Crazy things in my head. Like dumping my marriage crazy things. Any idea what that would cost me? This Dee Dee has me out of my mind. She has curly brown hair, unbelievable body, and sexy brown eyes. I would do anything for her. Then the woman with the blonde hair shows up at the dealership and all is ruined. A dagger in my heart would hurt less."

"Dee Dee her real name?"

"I thought. Not sure, now."

"Last name?"

"Daniels."

"She tell you anything about herself?"

"Yeah, lots."

"Believe her?"

He looked at me, and I could feel his disappointment. Suddenly he was no longer larger than life. He became a guy on my sofa with a pile of problems. Not everyday headaches like the rest of us, but problems just the same. My gut was my best friend when I worked a case, and now, my gut told me old Stan was being played.

"I do believe her. No doubt the blackmailer chick is someone involved with the Fantasy site—how else would they know about it, right? But yeah, Johnny, I believe Dee Dee."

"Or, Dee Dee told someone else and they decided to set themselves up for an easy payday."

"How could I be so stupid?"

"Stan, I have seen worse. You are not the first."

He nodded. "It's just...Dee Dee was special." He sunk further into the sofa.

"She could be innocent. You can never tell with these things."

"I hope."

"What do you want me to do?"

"Get me clear of this? Figure out a payoff or something? Hell, this can't blow up in my face. It will cost me much more than a hundred grand."

"I understand. Not much to go on, but we start with the website and Dee Dee. We can dig online, find out who owns the site, that sort of thing. When do you meet her again?"

"Tonight at my apartment."

I gave him the notepad. "Write down the address and the time. Your phone number. What else do you know about her? Where she lives? Anything?"

"Said she was from Port City, family moved around, came from nothing. Told me she didn't want to complicate things with her personal past. I asked plenty of times, but she always said she wanted to enjoy the moment, concentrate on the future and how amazing we would be together."

"Did you still pay her?"

He nodded. "Like I said, an idiot. You know, in a weird way, I felt like I was helping those girls. Dee Dee especially. As if I was rescuing them from a destructive lifestyle. I always tipped way more than I needed. Sounds stupid. Overpay the hookers to justify my behavior."

I almost felt sorry for the guy. He got himself sucked in deep. "Hey, shake it off. You made a bad play, but it is now first and ten again. A new set of downs. Give me a day or so. Don't breathe a word about this."

"What about the woman? Five days left."

"First things first. I will call you."

We stood and shook hands. "Thanks, Johnny. I appreciate this. Whatever it costs."

I walked with him down to the alley where he had parked his brand-new, royal-blue, Corvette Stingray.

"Now this is the way to go," I said.

"Midlife crisis written all over it. I'll send one over for you, whenever you want. One for Mike, too."

"Tempting, but I'm good for now."

He opened the car door. "You think I'm in trouble."

"Can't tell yet, but don't worry. We'll figure it out. The Shelton way."

He smiled and winked. "Damn right."

4

The Harbor Lofts building was part of a new collection of high-end retail shops, restaurants, offices, and apartment/condos all designed to revitalize the Port City Harbor area. The mayor and city leaders debated the merits of the development for years, but once the new Harbor Walk opened to great success, real estate values skyrocketed in the surrounding neighborhoods, and the mayor took full credit. Two celebrity chefs opened restaurants and the area became the hot nightlife destination for both locals and tourists.

The crowded streets also made it easy for me and Katie to be inconspicuous as we sat in my car and watched the entrance to the Harbor Lofts building—and Stan's love nest.

Hiding in plain sight. My BMW Z4 blended perfectly with the other luxury cars lining the street, and we even dressed for the part in case we needed to follow our target on foot. I wore a blazer with jeans and Katie had a skirt, heels, and full makeup. The modern day couple out for a night on the town.

"Do we know what she looks like?" She had a camera and a GPS tracking device on her lap.

"Stan will text me when she's close. Curly brown hair."

"That narrows it. What kind of car?"

"Not sure. Keep your eye on the door."

A little pre-case prep told me the Harbor Lofts building was all glass and steel with offices on the first four floors and condo apartments on floors six through ten. The rooftop had a gym and spa, a pool, cabanas, and a party area with gas grills for residents. Stan's apartment was a one-bedroom on the sixth.

Katie smoothed her skirt then checked her makeup in the visor mirror. "I love being dressed up for a job. Usually we're in jeans. This is much more exotic, like we are spies on an international mission."

"Tonight you're a Bond girl."

"Yes! I could be a double agent or something. I wish we could waltz into one of the restaurants, everyone's head turns, and they stare at us as we saunter up to the bar and order martinis. All the people would wonder about the sophisticated couple."

"Saunter?"

"Yeah, saunter in. Nothing but class, grace, and intrigue."

"Intrigue? Well, I say we do that, right after we conclude our business tonight."

"Serious?"

"Yep. Be a shame to waste how amazing you look."

"Aw, thank you, boss." She pointed to a building diagonal from the Harbor Lofts. "I heard that place is good. Mare e Monti."

"Yes, but we can do better. A new jazz club opened two blocks from here. The Blue Coral Lounge. More your Bond-girl style."

"My friend Mandy told me about it." She held up her hand for a high five. "I'm so excited. C'mon girl, whoever you are, we need to stick a tracker on your car and get on with our night."

The plan was to place a GPS device on Dee Dee's car so we could track her and see where she led us. Not ethical, but neither was working as a prostitute. The blackmailer had to be someone with inside knowledge of the business, which meant Dee Dee tipped off somebody about Stan and how loaded he was, or someone inside the business spotted him as a client.

She was to arrive at ten thirty p.m. Stan said she drove herself but sometimes used a car service. In that case, all we could do would be to try to snap a few photos.

At eleven, I traded text messages with Stan. He said she was never late and asked us to wait.

"Crazy how some of these guys get themselves in trouble. They have money, fame, and yet still manage to do dumb things to ruin it," Katie said.

"Ego takes over and they think they're immune to laws and normal human behavior. I have seen this a thousand times. If not for sex, greed, and inflated egos, we would be out of work."

"Disappointing, though. My dad put his autograph in a frame already. He worships the guy."

"Want to hear a dirty little secret?"

She twisted toward me in her seat. "You need to ask?"

"Do not tell your father. He would be devastated."

"Never. Ever. Tell me."

"Stan's career ended when he got injured. Huge deal, major headlines. At the top of his game, and all of a sudden, finished. The story was he broke his ankle during a private workout session before the season began. Keep your eye on the building."

"I am. Keep going."

"The secret? He never got hurt. They caught him gambling on his own games and the league did not want the embarrassment. So they created a cover-up to avoid all the negative press and to save Stan. He wore a fake cast for six weeks, went on TV crying about the end of his career, and drew sympathy from everyone."

"Wow. Nobody found out?"

"Officially, no. But it is the worst-kept secret. Stan would never admit it, or the league. They discovered many other players were gambling on games and did not want to face the pressure."

"Everything is a cover-up these days."

At eleven thirty, the traffic, both cars and pedestrians, began to thin. "Yep. Nothing is sacred anymore. I'm calling Stan." He answered on the first ring. "Is she coming? She call you?"

"No. I called her. No answer."

"We'll wait another—"

A black Chevrolet Suburban skidded to a halt in front of the building. A back door opened and a woman's body was tossed out to the road like a rag doll. The door slammed shut and the SUV peeled away.

Katie hit me on the arm. "Johnny, you see that? They just pushed her out."

The woman laid, motionless, on the pavement.

"Go, go. Take pictures." She jumped out with the camera as I put the phone to my ear. "Stan, I think your date is here."

5

A woman screamed and a mass of people circled the blonde girl lying on the pavement.

"Call 911!"

"They threw her out of the car."

"Damn, she's dead."

I kept Stan on the line as I opened my car door and stepped out. "Do you have a view of the street? Look out."

A moment passed. "What happened? Holy—"

"Not your girl, is it?"

"What? No—does that girl have blonde hair?"

"Yep."

"Johnny—?"

"I want you out of there. Where's your car?"

"The parking garage. What about Dee Dee?"

A man in the crowd shouted. *"Hey, quit with the pictures you sick pervert!"*

"Forget about her. Meet me at McNally's. In the alley." A siren flared in the distance. "Now, Stan."

I spotted Katie's blonde hair as she ran back to the car. We both hopped in and I started the engine.

"Holy shit. The girl's neck is broken, all twisted at this weird angle. Got to be dead," Katie said. "Could she be the escort?"

I eased my car from the parking spot and crept my way through the maze of onlookers gawking at the scene. "Get pictures?"

"Didn't you hear them yelling at me? I'm shaking." She held out a trembling hand. "Oh my God, some guy was screaming and a woman pushed me. First dead body I have ever seen, except for my grandmother, but she died when I was ten and I don't remember much—"

"The pictures?"

She scrolled through the photos. "Yes, good ones. I mean terrible, but the shots...she was pretty, too."

"Does she look like the girl Stan described?" I said, as we pulled to the side of the road to allow an ambulance and a police car to pass.

"No, not at all. Long blonde hair. He said brown and curly."

She handed me the camera and I went through the pictures. "This is no coincidence."

The blue Corvette was in the alley when we arrived. Stan got out of his car as I pulled mine into my garage. I had Katie usher him around the building and up to my condo while I went in McNally's through the kitchen door. Always one to make sure I had the right tools for the job, I grabbed a bottle of Scotch.

Mike was behind the bar, drying glasses and loading them on the rack. "Hey."

I pointed to the TV set on the wall. "Any chance you had on the local news?"

"No. Ball game. Why?"

"Shelton case just flipped upside down."

"Yeah? Fill me in."

"I will, as soon as I figure it out myself."

Stan paced nonstop from the front door to the balcony and back. He had his phone in his hand and had dialed Dee Dee for the eighth time. Katie had a laptop open on the kitchen table and was typing notes from the evening.

I poured drinks. "Sit down. You're making me nervous."

"She's not answering." He slipped the phone into his pocket. "She always answers." He pulled out a chair and sat, and I set a Scotch in front of him. "So you think the girl on the street has something to do with me? This can't be happening."

"No idea at this point. Did you hire Dee Dee through the website for tonight?"

"Yes. Told me she would be fired if she were to agree to a date outside the site. We talked about her quitting. I wanted her to be exclusive to me."

"We need to talk about the woman—the blackmailer—who came to your office." I showed him the pictures on the camera.

"Yeah, I think that's her," he said. "Oh my God." He threw back the whiskey and I poured more.

"Can you remember anything else about her? Did you see what she drove? Anyone with her?"

"No. Nothing. Remember, I thought some guy was coming to talk to me about being a spokesman for their company." His knee pumped up and down like a jackhammer going through concrete. I worried he would fall apart if I didn't give him some reassurance. "I'm an idiot. I knew my behavior would eventually destroy me."

"No time for self-pity. I need you to think." I put a hand on his arm. "Let's work through this, talk through the angles. From my experience, the more we explore who knew what, the easier it is to figure out what happened."

He turned the glass around in his hands. His eyes went from me to Katie, and back. "You're the boss."

Katie cleared her throat, sat up in her chair. Time to be an investigator. "Did Dee Dee ever talk about anybody else involved with the site? Any other escorts, any friends? Do you know if she had to meet anyone in person to work for Fantasy? An interview?"

He shook his head. "No, we never talked about it. Once I asked how long she did this...kind of work. She said less than a year. I did wonder about how she got paid because I wanted to pay her cash, which she refused. Said she didn't want to break the rules."

"Her pay was sent to her bank account?"

"Yes, I guess. Wait—she did mention one time she was scared of the woman who hired her. Said she was afraid to get on her bad side."

"She say anything else about her? Who she was or how she got the job?"

"No. Again, I never asked."

"Go back to the day when the woman came to your work," Katie asked.

"I said all I know."

"A man called you first, right?"

Stan nodded.

"Did his voice sound familiar?"

"No," he said.

"Did he call your cell phone or an office line?"

"Cell."

"So someone gave him your cell number."

"I can't believe this." He finished off his second drink, slumped back in the chair, and closed his eyes. The booze and the emotions of the night were an anchor pulling him under. Katie asked the right questions, but he was of no help.

I cleared the bottle and glasses. "C'mon, Stan. Time to head home." I grabbed his arm and helped him up. "I'll drive you. Katie will follow us."

"Horseshit. I can drive." He yanked his arm from me, turned, and stumbled over his chair and fell to the floor. We managed to stand him upright again. "Damn, I really screwed up this time, didn't I?"

"Stan, don't worry. We'll sort this out." I was behind him with both hands on his shoulders steering him toward the door. "Plus, it gives me a chance to drive the Corvette."

6

Paul Ellison was the detective who caught the case of the murdered girl thrown from the SUV, and it only took Mike two phone calls and a promise of free drinks for life to extract information on the murder. They were rookie cops together over twenty-five years ago on the PCPD, and although Paul was reluctant to divulge any details, as he should be, Mike gently reminded him of the times he covered for him when he got juiced up while on duty. He agreed to stop by McNally's and was on time at ten.

If I had met him on the street, I might not have recognized him. What remained of his hair was white-gray and he carried at least an extra thirty pounds, most of it packed around the middle, and now wore wire-framed glasses that rested halfway down his nose. He and Mike crowded beside each other in the booth like two white sardines crammed in a can. I worried the bench would collapse.

"Something wrong with a table?" Ellison smirked.

"And miss this lovely moment with you two? I should take a picture."

"Go to hell."

Katie came over and poured coffees while Ellison's eyes traveled the length of her body. His eyes popped when she came back with a notepad and sat beside me.

"Who's this?"

"My investigator. Katie."

"You're a PI?"

She shook his hand. "Working on it. My pleasure, Detective."

He looked at Mike with arched eyebrows and an old-school "why is a woman invading our sacred club" attitude.

"All good," Mike said.

"Man, the next thing you know, they'll allow women to vote."

Mike asked Katie, "Would you mind getting a bottle of Jack Daniels?"

"Now?"

"Please."

She got up from the booth, went to the bar, and came back with a bottle.

I poured a shot's worth into Ellison's coffee, but he slid his cup back to me as if I offended him. I added another dose of truth serum.

"Much better." Ellison aimed at my blonde assistant. "The woman's name was Kendra Fitzgerald. Went by Kenzie. Thirty-three. Worked as a high-class escort. One of the expensive hookers Mike could never afford."

"How do you know this?" I asked.

"Policeman's salary. Hell, he couldn't afford the twenty-dollar hooker on the corner."

"Funny, Paul. Real funny." Mike handed the whiskey to Katie. "Put it back."

"C'mon, haven't seen you guys in forever. I need to take a few jabs. Lose your sense of humor?"

"All right, keep talking." Mike grabbed the bottle from Katie and poured another slug in Paul's coffee.

"Bank records. She received weekly deposits from a company, Entertainment Ventures, LLC, doing business as Fantasy Escorts."

"The same site. Wow." Katie jotted notes. I nudged her knee with mine and hoped she understood the universal "shut up" signal.

"You know it?" Ellison asked. "Remember, the information flows both ways here."

"In due time," I said.

He sipped his coffee with a stink eye pointed at me. "Anyhow, the ME confirmed the broken neck, probably killed somewhere else."

"Any priors?"

"Two minors, both for solicitation."

"When did she start with Entertainment Ventures?"

"Eighteen months ago."

"When are you releasing her name to the press?" I asked.

"So far we can't find any family. Once we do, and they are notified, we'll release. Hopefully tonight or tomorrow at the latest."

"What about the SUV?"

"First shows up on street cameras three blocks away from the dump spot. Plates reported stolen last month. My turn to ask the questions."

"Goes no further than this cozy little booth. Can't afford you getting tanked and yapping about our case." Paul was a functioning drunk for the past twenty years but always managed his case load and closed as many cases as the young, eager detectives. His financial support of the whiskey distilleries never diminished his ability to work the street, nor cost him any respect of colleagues. And, he could be trusted.

"I'm insulted you would think that of me." He waved a hand. "Nobody listens to me anymore, anyhow. They all consider me past my time. A washed-up old detective waiting to retire or die. There is an office pool on which one happens first."

"Enough of the boo-hoo," Mike said. Katie giggled.

Ellison pushed his glasses up on his nose and focused on me. "So, why the interest?"

"Let's say we have a high-profile client who partakes of Fantasy's website."

"Gee, I'm shocked. A rich guy hiring high-class hookers. What's the world coming to?" He started to raise his cup to his mouth but stopped. "So, the dead girl was your client's date?"

"No, not exactly."

"Either she was or she wasn't."

"She was not his date."

"You sure? Because I'm confused. You ask me here for information on the girl, most of which you could get from the evening news tonight, and—" He let go of his coffee cup and sat back in the booth. "If she was not his date, what led you to believe the victim would connect to your client?" He studied me for a second and then shifted his gaze to Katie, then back to me. His detective brain fired on all cylinders; his head bobbed up and down. "Either your client was there, or he knew the girl, or you were there with your client for some reason and you saw this go down. How am I doing? C'mon, Johnny, why am I here?"

Did I take this too far? I figured he would probe, ask why we wanted information. I did not want to give up the real blackmail angle just yet, but I needed to feed him something. He would know instantly if I held back. Plus, any detective would kill for a juicy extortion case involving a celebrity. Even a minor celeb.

"My client hired girls from the site. He got attached to one in particular and hired her multiple times. She told him she fell in love with him, wanted him to divorce his wife, said she wanted to quit the business so they could move in together. Naturally, he gets nervous, fears she is going to do something crazy and screw up his life."

"She's setting him up for a payday."

"My first thought, too. He wanted us to investigate, find out who she really was, then slip between her and the scheme she was cooking. He was to meet her at the new Italian place..." I turned to Katie for help.

"Mare e Monti. Received excellent reviews," she said.

Thank God she was on my wavelength, validating my story with the name of the restaurant.

"Yep. On the corner. I wanted to snap a few pics, try to spot her car, license plate, whatever. From there, they were headed to a hotel. Ten minutes before they were to meet, the SUV pulls in front of us, the door opens, and the girl is dropped. I called my client and told him to leave the area. Then we split. He later said his girl never showed or called. Gut instinct kicked in, got me curious, and we called you."

"The two of you left the scene."

"Cops were responding, plenty of witnesses."

"So you just happened to be parked on the street right where Ms. Fitzgerald was dumped." Ellison pulled a notepad from his jacket. "The vic was not your guy's date, but she worked for the same service as his go-to girl? What a coincidence."

"Right, and I'm asking you keep it to yourself. For now."

"Why? You owe him something?"

"No. Deep inside, he's a stand-up guy. People love him, and I would hate to see him crash and burn over this. His own fault, but it would be a real disappointment to many people if word got out."

He elbowed Mike. "Now he has a heart?"

"What can I say? Miracles happen," Mike said. "Paul, we are asking as colleagues. Plus all the booze you want is on the house. Give him a few days. For old time's sake."

"The gut." I patted my belly. "You know what I mean. Detective's instinct, and mine is telling me someone—"

"Sent your boy a message. Whoever killed the girl knew where your client was meeting his date."

"Exactly."

He wagged a finger at me and shook his head. "How about this: your wealthy big shot of a client just whacked a potential blackmailer. Are you receiving that message?"

I glanced at Katie and she was scribbling away: ...*whacked...blackmail...sending a message.*

"My client didn't whack anyone. Guaranteed."

"If you say so."

"Why would he hire me?"

"All right, you got a point," he said. "Why am I here again?"

"After last night I'm afraid my guy got himself mixed up with some bad people. He's no saint, but I don't want his name in the paper if it doesn't have to be. Here's the deal: you give me what you got, and I'll do the same. If I'm wrong and he's dirty, he's all yours."

The old grizzled detective studied me for a second and then checked my partner.

"For a few days," Mike said.

Paul nodded. "You have a few days. Anything begins to stink, the deal is off. Plus, I get the collar on the homicide."

"Yep," I said.

"Now let me out of this booth. I'm claustrophobic."

We all slid out and Ellison took Katie's hand. "Be careful. No place for a girl. Except these two jokers will make you a pro. Best in the biz."

She beamed.

Paul grabbed a bottle of Jack Daniels from behind the bar. "This will keep me quiet for a while."

Mike turned to me as we watched him leave. "We should send him a case."

7

Once a month, twenty-five or so ex-cops, all members of the local chapter of the Fraternal Order of Police come in to McNally's for a meeting. In reality, it is ten minutes of business discussion and two hours to drink beer and shoot the shit. Mike and Katie busied themselves preparing for the group and Carlos Suarez, our part-time bartender and cook, came in to assist. A sergeant on the PCPD, he picked up extra cash by working a shift or two on the weekends plus he covered the monthly FOP gathering.

I hustled up to my condo, dialing Stan on the way. His voice mail picked up. "Stan, I need you to call me right away." It was the third message I had left for him since we met with Paul Ellison forty minutes earlier. I needed him to be where I could see or talk to him at all times, at least until I formulated a strategy for this case. I gathered a writing tablet, a blank manila folder, and my laptop and headed back to the bar.

The tables were filled, and the business portion of the meeting was underway. I waved Katie over to join me.

"Sit. Guess what we forgot," I said.

She wiped her hands on her apron and sat across from me in the booth. "What?"

"Lucky for us, Ellison did not hold back information, but he only answered what we asked."

"Yeah?"

"What was the one piece of vital data we missed?"

Her brow furrowed. "Umm, he gave us her name, age, employer, how long she worked there." She shrugged. "Said she had two priors, and we need more background. Her friends and associates."

"Kenzie's address."

"Oh, right. That was dumb."

"Let it be a lesson. My mistake, too. He had me focused on Stan and how he could be jammed in this mess, and I forgot the basics. So, never forget." I ticked them off on my fingers. "Name, address, date of birth, phone number. On me too, but I want you to learn."

She untied a ponytail and let her hair fall. "I understand. I'm on it as soon as Mike frees me up. Should be easy to find from the databases. I do have a question. Why *did* you call Detective Ellison? He even said what he told us would be on the news and I'm sure he knows we can find out where she worked and all, including her address."

"To protect our client. For as long as we can. Paul is a smart, thorough detective and if he decides the girl's murder is somehow connected to her employer, he'll have the DA subpoena Fantasy's records. The site's lawyers will argue against it—but eventually Stan will be outed as a client. Plus, we get information. He told us the parent company is Entertainment Ventures because they pulled her bank accounts. Which is something we can't do. If

Paul can funnel information to us before it hits the street, we might be able to drag Stan out of this. He gave us some time, so you know what you need to do."

"Yep, find everything we can on Kenzie, plus the mysterious Dee Dee, the call girl who stole Stan's heart." She re-tied her ponytail. "Sounds like a bad romance novel."

"I'd love to find out why she didn't show up for the date last night."

"You think she's behind the blackmailing, don't you?"

A collective cheer went up from the FOP guys.

"Hey, Stan the man!"

Katie and I both stood, and there in the middle of the bar, surrounded by all the retired cops, was the king of the gridiron himself. He was in his element. Handshakes, back slaps, and hugs all around. He signed autographs and posed for more than enough selfies, often taking the camera and snapping the picture himself. The cops all knew the real story behind Stan, but it never stopped anyone from basking in the presence of football greatness. Sports fans have a way of forgiving and his glory days on the field far outweighed his indiscretions. Beers and shots were shoved in front of Stan, and he gladly obliged.

"Go over there and get him." I nudged Katie. "Need to keep him sober."

Stan spotted her as she approached the group of men and threw an arm around her.

"Gentlemen, isn't she the finest specimen of a woman you have ever seen?" He ran his hand through her hair. "The sexy hair, the baby blues, and those legs. Ever see legs like this? They go from the floor clear up to the Promised Land."

Katie's face and neck turned crimson as the men laughed.

"She can come home with me anytime!" "I want to go to the Promised Land."

She slipped out from under Stan's arm. "C'mon, Mr. Shelton, we need you in back."

"Boys, I gotta go. Can you blame me? She said she needs me on my back." More laughs. "I would follow that fine filly anywhere." The men were all up and shaking Stan's hand. "Be back as soon as I can." He called to Mike. "Their drinks are on me. Anything for my cop friends. Toughest people I know. Real heroes."

Another cheer went up from the crowd as Katie hurried over to me. "What an arrogant, gross, vile pig. I have never been so humiliated."

"Shake it off. Other pressing matters."

Stan made it to my booth, leaving his impromptu fan club in his wake.

"Why didn't you answer my calls? I tried all morning." I pushed him down into the booth and sat across from him.

"Hey, relax, Johnny boy. All is good."

"How so?"

"Dee Dee called me late last night. She's safe, so I'm happy. It's all cool."

"Not cool, Stan. Did you forget about the girl thrown from the car? The one you said came to your office? We confirmed she's connected to the Fantasy site. Last night we suspected—today we know. If the cops gain access to records from the website, how long do you think it will be before they stumble across your name?"

He sat there with a dumb bewilderment crowding his face.

"Why didn't Dee Dee show up for your date last night?" I asked.

"Said she wasn't feeling well, took some cold medicine and fell asleep."

"You believe her?"

"Yeah, Johnny. I believe her. Why would you ask me—"

"Stan, we don't know who or what to believe right now. For me to keep you out of this, you need to do what I say, and that includes answering your phone. Now go wait in the kitchen. We're going up to my condo."

"Sorry. I was so happy that she called—"

"Now."

He went into the kitchen, and I pulled Katie aside. "Tell Mike I need you and take Stan upstairs. Don't worry about what he said. If you are going to be a woman in a man's world, the worst is yet to come. You need a tough skin."

She nodded. "I understand. He's so gross, though. Such a sick perv."

"It is all about the eternal quest of man. Goes back thousands of years."

"What?"

She was annoyed but I could not resist. "Every man's quest to get to the Promised Land."

"Really? You think that is funny? I'm the one who has to go wait on those guys."

"Maybe you should wear a housecoat and hair net from now on?"

"Now you're sick and perverted."

8

Carlos had taken a bag of trash to the bin in the alley and was coming back in through the kitchen as I was headed out.

"Boss, wait," he said. "You expecting company?"

"Why?"

"Black Jeep Cherokee with black rims at the end of the alley. Been there for a while." He held up his phone with a picture of the car and the plate number. "Sending it to you now."

"How many in the car?"

"One woman. Brown hair. Thirties, maybe."

"Great work, thanks. We'll be upstairs."

"Sure. Hey, is Stan Shelton your client?"

"Yes, and keep that to yourself."

"Copy that, chief. I was always a fan."

He went on his way, and I turned around and went through the bar and out the front. I remembered why I always used the back stairs and it was not for the exercise—the elevator in the residential side of the building was so slow Stan could shoot a car commercial in the time it took to travel the four floors to my condo.

He was parked at the table with his cell phone cradled between his head and shoulder and a small day planner opened in front of him. He jotted in the notebook as he confirmed appointments.

I looked to Katie, who had a pot of coffee brewing.

"His agent." She leaned against the kitchen counter with her arms folded across her chest.

Over the past few months of getting to know her, I had become adept in reading her moods. Adept as any man could be at reading a woman's mood, which was lousy at best. I slid beside her and whispered, "You don't have to like the client."

She cocked an eyebrow at me.

"We want to help most of the people who hire us. They are usually victims—being cheated on or taken advantage of. We want to help them because we see the ugly side of life and want them to get what they rightly deserve. Stan is different. He hired prostitutes and cheated on his wife, which makes him despicable in some eyes, maybe yours, but he hired us because he is being blackmailed, and that makes *him* a victim. Like I told Paul, Shelton has a good heart and is not a bad guy. Only arrogant, crass, crude, and creepy." That drew a smile. "Are you ready to work?"

She shrugged. "I guess."

"There is a black Jeep Cherokee in the alley. Might be a tail on Stan."

"Serious?"

I showed her my phone with the picture of the license number. "Are we good?"

"Hell, yeah."

Stan ended his phone call. "Sorry, Johnny. I should have answered your calls last night, but I was overjoyed Dee Dee was okay. Had to go out and celebrate."

"You now need to be a hermit. Stay home, limit the personal appearances, banquets, golf tournaments, whatever else you got lined up—"

"Wait. Can I say something?" He pushed back from the table, stood, and faced Katie. "Miss Katie, I embarrassed you down in the bar, and I want to apologize. When I'm in groups like that, guys expect me to be...a certain way." He held up his hands in surrender. "I used you in the moment and it was disrespectful, and I'm sorry."

I had not expected him to apologize and neither did Katie, judging from the fact she was almost speechless. She was never speechless.

"Oh, um...sure, I accept your apology."

"Thanks. I take it we need to talk?"

"Yep. Sit," she said. He pulled a chair out for her and sat beside her as she opened her computer. I poured coffees.

"Stan, know anyone who drives a black Cherokee with black rims?" I asked.

Katie's fingers flew over her keyboard, running a search on the car and plate.

"No, nothing comes to mind."

I paced around the kitchen. "You came to me because you were being blackmailed. A few days later, the girl who came to your office was murdered and dumped at your feet." I tapped on the table. "Message killing."

"Message? Jesus, Johnny." He rubbed his hand across his jaw and leaned back in the chair. "I don't understand...message about what? The blackmail?"

"No idea, but don't think the blackmail is over. You tell anyone else about this?"

"No, I swear."

"You could be mixed up with some real nasty people. You are a public figure. You have money—they know it—and now you made yourself vulnerable. Maybe someone knew about the girl approaching you and decided to double down on the blackmail."

"How so?"

"They remove her from the equation and then come at you for more money. Set you up for murder unless you pay."

"Damn, Johnny. I didn't do anything."

"You did when you hired escorts. You inserted yourself into the world of prostitutes, drug dealers, thugs, and gangsters. Where do you think those girls come from? Huh? Strip clubs. Massive amounts of drugs go through those places. Those girls are all hooked. High on money and drugs. They make a lot dancing, quickly learn how much more they can make by turning tricks. Then the hot ones figure out they can make even more as a high-end escort. More money, better drugs."

"Dee Dee doesn't do drugs."

"Stan, the point is, these are desperate, heartless people who will do anything. They dumped a dead girl in the middle of a crowded street, for God's sake. All they care about is money."

"I got something," Katie said.

I sat at the table and she turned her computer to me.

"Anthony DeRenzo. Sound familiar?" I asked.

"DeRenzo?" The blood drained from Stan's face. "That's Dee Dee's real last name."

"Stan—" Katie and I glared at him.

"Sorry."

"We'll address that later. There was a black Jeep Cherokee in the alley just now. Registered to an Anthony DeRenzo. Did Dee Dee ever talk about an Anthony?"

"No. Never. I don't understand."

"Ever mention a brother? Cousin?"

"No."

"I got a birthdate. He is forty-two," Katie said.

Stan raised his hands and shrugged.

"You need to stay home until we figure this out. No events, no going out for dinners, nothing. Stay out of the public eye," I said.

"I can't do that. My agent books my appearances. What would I say? In fact, I'm shooting a promo spot at the dealership in an hour."

"Can you come back here after the shoot?"

"Nikki and I are going to a fundraiser tonight for the hospital. How about I drop her off at the house after and then come back?"

"No, on second thought, go straight home after your event. And stay there. Call me first thing in the morning."

"You're the boss." He took a deep breath. "Please tell me you'll figure this out."

"We will, but you need to do what I say. Is there anything else you're not telling us?"

"No. I promise." He got up from the table and stood before Katie. "I was sincere in my apology, and I want you to know you are way more attractive than any of the hookers I've hired. You could make a fortune as an escort."

I couldn't blame her if she had lashed out with a kick to his groin. Instead, a small half-smile sort of leaked across her face. She nodded and went back to the computer.

He walked out.

She kept her focus on the laptop. "I dare you to say one word."

9

"You won't believe it." Katie yanked me from behind the bar and pulled me to the back booth. She opened her computer. "Anthony DeRenzo's car and Entertainment Ventures use the same address."

"Well, what do you know?"

"Also, he has two priors for possession with intent to distribute."

"He sounds like an upstanding citizen. I say we put eyeballs on the place. Meet you at my car in ten."

Entertainment Ventures, LLC, was located in an old business park on the west side of Port City called, the Commons. The complex was made up of one-story cinder block buildings, each having six separate businesses. The units had an office entrance in the front and a loading area in the back. Entertainment Ventures was in the first six-unit structure, sandwiched between Gary's Auto Body and Amazing Graphics, a T-shirt design shop. We circled around the rear of the building and only the body shop had their large roll-up door open.

Back on the access road, we parked fifty yards away with an unobstructed view of the office door. I twisted a long lens on my Nikon and snapped shots of the building. Katie did a deep dive into Anthony DeRenzo and came up with a Twenty-Seventh Street address.

"That's a few blocks from where I grew up. Near Little Italy," I said.

"It's the most current address I can find on him—wait, check this out. When I go back on his previous addresses, there is a Daniella DeRenzo. Same address. Daniella has to be Dee Dee." She punched my arm. "Damn, I am so awesome. Could be brother and sister?"

"Now we are making progress. Good work."

"But why would Stan say Dee Dee's last name was Daniels?"

"Protecting her." Telling Katie he was protecting Dee Dee was true, but my gut was telling me Stan could be protecting himself. What else had Stan not told us?

"Oh, yeah. I forgot he's in love."

"Or they could be husband and wife."

"Which means Anthony was pimping out his wife. Scumbag. Stan would be devastated."

"Wouldn't surprise me a bit." I clicked off more pics of the building and cars in the lot. "Recap."

"Okay. So, Daniella is Dee Dee—which is my guess— and we assume Anthony is her brother, and since he uses the Entertainment Ventures address, it could mean he's the owner?"

"Could be. But we're not going to find out anything by sitting here. I say we begin with the neighbors."

We drove around the building to Gary's Auto Body. We parked and walked to the open garage door.

A small Hispanic man wearing a mask and coveralls was sanding the hood of a blue Camaro. He stopped when we approached.

I flashed my investigator's ID. "The owner around?"

He gave us both a once-over and pointed to the front of the shop.

We tiptoed our way through a minefield of sanders, buckets, and spray-painting equipment and found a tall, lanky, white guy leaning on a counter, flipping through pages on a clipboard. He had earbuds planted in his ears and I shouted to announce us. "Excuse me."

He yanked out the earphones. "Sorry about that. Name's Gary. How can I help you?" He wiped off his hand with a rag and extended it but pulled it back when I held up my license.

"Doing a background investigation on your neighbor. Entertainment Ventures. Can we ask you a few questions?"

He looked at Katie then back to me. "What kind of background?" He folded his arms across his chest.

"They applied for a government contract."

"Contract?"

I sensed his skepticism. "All routine. We'll only take a minute."

He shrugged. "I don't know nothing anyhow. Go ahead."

"What type of business are they in? Seems quiet."

"No idea what they do. Except for the one gal, hardly anyone ever goes in the place."

I pulled a pen and notepad from my pocket. More for show than anything else. "Our information said they're event planners. Any trucks or vans ever come by?"

He shook his head. "If they are doing events, they don't do it from here. Like I said, we only see the one girl." He focused on Katie more than me but who could blame him?

"Can you describe her?" I asked.

"Yeah. Tall, with long, black hair. Only met her once. Locked her keys in her car and came in to use the phone. We called her Pocahontas. Because of the hair. Good-looking, too." His face turned red as he glanced at Katie. "Real exotic type. Drives a green Jaguar."

"Exotic? What do you mean?"

"Umm...different. Light skin. My guess is she's mixed. Part black, part white or part something else."

"You catch her name?"

"No. Don't *you* have her name?"

"Yes, but we hoped you could confirm what was on the application. Anything else you can think of? Employees?"

"Nah, no—wait, the muscle guy."

"Muscle guy?"

"Weightlifter type. Comes around every now and then. We made fun of him because he wore the same thing every time we saw him. Black jeans and a black muscle shirt. Gold chains around his neck, hair slicked back. Not very tall but real cut. Wouldn't want to mess with the dude. Hector, my employee, called him a poser."

"A poser?"

Katie jumped in. "A wannabe, a phony."

"Okay. I'm hip," I said.

They both laughed.

"Yeah, one of those guys who's all show. Looks tough but really isn't," he said.

"Happened to notice what he drives?"

He thought for a second. "Nah, I don't remember. Too many cars come through here. Can't keep them all straight."

"Fair enough. Thank you for your time. Appreciate it." This time I extended a hand and he shook it.

"Don't know if I was much help."

"Hey, every bit helps."

He reached out and took Katie's hand. "Ever need any body work done, give me a call."

We got back in the car and she opened her laptop to make notes on the interview. "All I have is a woman who they call Pocahontas because of long black hair and she drives a green Jag," she said.

"He liked you," I said.

"Who?"

"Gary, of Gary's Auto Body."

"No he didn't."

"Body work? He wasn't talking about cars—"

Tires squealed and our heads jerked to the road. A green Jaguar F-Type fishtailed around the corner, shot past us—missing my car by inches—turned in to the lot, and parked in front of Entertainment Ventures.

"Damn, Johnny! Almost hit us."

"The green Jag. Maybe it's her." I picked up my camera just as the driver's door opened. Out stepped a tall, slender woman wearing a white business suit and white heels. She had long, straight black hair that fell halfway down her back. She locked the car with the key fob, and then turned toward us and stared. I kept clicking off pictures and hoped we were too far away for her to get a look at us—or my license plate. After a long couple of seconds, she unlocked the door to Entertainment Ventures and went in. I snapped a shot of her license plate.

"Must be her." Katie grabbed the camera from my hand and scrolled through the pictures. "She's gorgeous. Pocahontas in the flesh. I wonder how much she makes if she's one of the escorts."

She zoomed in on a shot of the woman staring at us. From what I could tell from the small screen, the woman had light-brown skin and high cheek bones.

I couldn't agree more.

Gorgeous.

10

We made two passes of the Twenty-Seventh Street address of Dee Dee and Anthony DeRenzo before parking a half-block away. It was a fairly quiet street of row homes on the edge of Little Italy. Strictly an Italian area when I grew up in this part of town, but it appeared many of the homes were getting makeovers in a now diverse, hip, and gentrifying neighborhood. It gave me an idea.

Katie and I talked through a plan and I called her cell with instructions for her to keep the line open so I could listen to any conversation. With her notebook and phone in hand, she got out and walked up to the house. She knocked on the door.

No answer. She tried again. "Nobody home," she said.

"Okay, come on back. No wait, a lady is coming." An older woman, wearing a light-blue housecoat and a gray button-up sweater, shuffled along the sidewalk toward the house. She pulled a two-wheeled wire cart loaded with bags of groceries.

The woman stopped at the row house. "Whatever you're selling, I'm not buying."

Katie extended her hand which the lady ignored. "Hello. My name is Amber and I'm with Port City

Windows. We are doing some work two blocks over. I was talking to several of the neighbors and wanted to ask if you've considered having your windows replaced. Many of the homes in this area are getting to the point where the windows should be upgraded."

"Not interested."

Katie made a show of looking at her notebook. "You must be Mrs. DeRenzo, right?"

The woman cocked an eyebrow at her. "How do you know my name?"

"Oh, these marketing companies give me a list of everyone's name and address. Nothing is private anymore."

"That, I agree with. My phone doesn't stop ringing with people trying to sell me something. Between them and the church, everyone wants money."

"Those calls are so annoying, aren't they?"

"You're in my way."

"I'm sorry." Katie stepped to the side. "Can I help you with those?"

"No." She pulled keys from her dress pocket and propped open an outer screen door with the cart of groceries.

"Can I ask you one more thing?"

"No."

"Not about windows. You look familiar. I think I've been here before. My older sister used to have a friend and I think this was her house. Daniella, maybe?"

The lady turned to her. "I never want to hear her name."

"I'm sorry, I didn't mean...is she your daughter?"

The woman turned her back to Katie and opened her door just as a black Jeep Cherokee pulled to the curb in front of the house. A man got out, wearing all black—jeans, boots, and muscle shirt. His black hair was slicked back. I snapped off a few photos.

"Ma, you okay? Who's this?" he yelled, as he headed to the house. His voice came through loud and clear through the phone.

"Somebody selling stuff. Told her I'm not buying."

He approached and Katie stuck out her hand. "Hi, my name is Amber and I'm with Port City Windows and we—"

The man brushed by her. "I don't give a shit who you're with. My mother said she is not buying. Get off our property."

"Sure. Sorry."

He scooped up the groceries and followed his mother inside. The door slammed. Katie hurried back to my car. "Got to be Anthony, right?" she said.

"Sure fits the description." My camera was to my eye and focused on the Cherokee's license plate. I read off the number.

She opened her notebook. "Yep. Matches the number Carlos gave us when he spotted the car in the alley. We can confirm he is Anthony and he owns the car—"

"No. All we can confirm is the black Cherokee is the same car that was in the alley, and owned by one Anthony

DeRenzo. We have not confirmed the charming gentleman you just met is Anthony. He probably is, but deal in facts, not assumptions."

"Well—the gentleman—fits the description of the guy who works at Entertainment Ventures and could be Daniella's brother."

"Or husband."

"I refuse to believe it, but okay." She tapped her pen on the paper.

"Katie, what we do is collect pieces to a puzzle. Then we take those pieces and move them around until something fits. Anthony is another piece. All under the scope of why we were hired."

"To find out who tried to blackmail Stan Shelton."

"Yep."

"And the murder of Kenzie in front of his building?"

"We're not investigating the murder, but years of experience tell me that solving one will solve the other."

"You called it a message job."

"Dumping the body in front of Stan's building—" I let it hang so she could move the pieces.

She wrote notes as she spoke. "To tell Stan the blackmail is over...or to tell him to keep quiet...or to tell him he needs to cooperate." Her big blue eyes looked to me for confirmation.

"They also risked being identified or caught."

"So sending the message outweighed the risk," she said.

"Yep." I started the car. "So, who gives us the most information?"

She thought for a second, scanned through her notes, and then pointed to a name in the notebook.

"Exactly."

11

"We're in a relationship. I don't care what you say."

"Mike, she only calls you when her kids are out of the house and she is alone. You never go out in public," Katie said.

We were back at McNally's. Katie tended bar as Mike was about to leave on an errand. An errand named Abby Lane. He met her two months ago at a policemen's benefit golf tournament and now had himself infatuated. We called her Abby Road, but Katie didn't understand the Beatle's reference and rolled her eyes when we explained. Whenever he said he needed to check something on Abby Road, we understood what he meant. He claimed he was now in a "friends with benefits" relationship, which Katie tried to explain the entire point was that it was not a relationship.

"So."

"She only wants one thing from you. Sex. That's the benefits part."

"Not all sex. We talk."

"You're her side dude. Whenever she has a need, she calls and off you go."

I laughed. Mike threw a bar towel at her. "She's not like that."

"You haven't met her children, have you?" Katie jabbed.

"No. Too complicated at the moment."

"All I'm saying is, be careful. She's going through a messy divorce. Abby Road could have potholes."

"Ha, she's on a roll tonight," I said. "Yeah, Mike, you might break your drive shaft."

Abby Lane was in the middle of divorcing Elliott Lane, currently a captain in the Port City Police Department. Elliott had found his own "friend with benefits" in the shape of his secretary. The scandal spread through the department faster than a wildfire on a dry California hillside, leaving Abby and her three teenage daughters alone in their large house. She met Mike while volunteering at the golf tournament and a week later, he was the friend reaping the benefits. I figured he was her personal revenge against her husband, but I couldn't hammer that through Mike's head.

He drew off a half-glass of draft beer and chugged it down. He pointed at Katie. "I'll deal with you tomorrow."

She threw the towel back at him. He dodged it and left in a huff as two customers entered and plopped down at the bar. Katie waited on them and I went to my booth and continued the research on Kenzie Fitzgerald. Katie had it right when she pointed to Kenzie's name in her notes. The dead girl had all the answers. All we had to do was figure out how to make her talk.

Every ten minutes Katie would come back to the booth, turn the computer from me, and check on my progress, which was not much.

"Let's trade." I went behind the bar while she sat and worked on the Kenzie research. The night crept along. Eleven thirty rolled around, and I glanced over at the booth and saw Katie curled up on the bench. It had been a long day, starting with Stan that morning.

The two guys at the bar were glued to a Yankees game going into the twelfth inning. I told them it was time to lockup, picked up their last round, and shooed them out over their protests, locking the door behind them.

I nudged Katie and it took her a second to wake up.

"Oh my God, I am so sorry." She stretched, yawned, and picked up the laptop. "I will work some more at home."

I took it from her. "No. You need sleep. I don't want you in before eleven tomorrow."

"Thank you. I'm exhausted."

We went through the kitchen and out to the alley where she parked. I waited until she pulled off. In light of the uncertainty of the Shelton case, at no point did I want her to be alone. Day or night. I did not tell Katie, but it bothered me that Anthony DeRenzo saw her. She was too easy to remember.

"Mr. Delarosa?"

A woman's voice. Behind me.

I wheeled around and instinctively reached for the gun on my hip, which I never wear in the restaurant. A reaction from years as a cop. A light was mounted above our door, but the rest of the alley was too dark for me to make out a person. I stayed quiet.

She stepped out from a shadow. "Mr. Delarosa?"

"Do I know you?"

"I'm sorry to bother you. I'm a friend of Stan Shelton. My name is Dee Dee."

"Dee Dee?" I did another check up and down the alley. Nothing.

"Can I talk to you?"

"What are you doing out here?"

"Waiting for you."

"Why?"

"I want to hire you. I want you to find out who killed Kenzie."

12

I grabbed Dee Dee's hand, and pulled her into the kitchen and locked the door behind us. "Don't move." The lights were still on in the bar, so I turned them off, then came back and snapped off the kitchen lights except for a small one over the range.

"How did you get here?" I asked.

"Took a cab. I didn't want to chance driving."

"Why hide in the alley?"

"Stan told me to keep it a secret that he hired you. If I came into the bar, people could see us." She kept her arms folded across her chest and stammered a bit when she talked. She was nervous or scared. Or both.

"What if I never came out?"

"He mentioned you live upstairs. I figured you would come out sooner or later."

"You tell anyone you were coming here?"

"No, nobody. I swear."

"Not Stan?"

"No way. He would be upset if he found out I was here."

Surprises were never my thing, and her showing up like this made *me* nervous and scared. Someone killed

Kenzie Fitzgerald and tossed her body in the street like a piece of litter. Anyone capable of that would not think twice about killing another high-class escort—or a second-rate private eye.

I unlocked the door and peeked into the alley. All quiet. I cursed myself for never installing security cameras in the back. *Add that to my mental to-do list.* "We'll go up to my place. Follow me."

We climbed the back stairs and entered the condo. Inside, I locked the door and pointed to a chair at the kitchen table. "Wait there." The living room had a sliding glass door that opened to my balcony and I did not want her anywhere near a window. I pulled the draperies across the door and turned on a lamp. "So, why are you here?"

"I'm scared, and I don't know who to talk to. Stan told me about you helping with the blackmail threat and I thought you could help with Kenzie."

What else had Stan told her? "Kenzie?"

"She was my friend. I can't believe she's dead. We used to be roommates, and she got me my job."

"At the escort service?"

She nodded and turned away, as if suddenly embarrassed by what she did for a living. I understood Stan's attraction, though. She was medium height with curves in all the right places. Curly brown hair fell to her shoulders and her golden-brown eyes had a warmth to them that was inviting and unguarded. The women in her business, even the top-dollar girls, usually had the markings of a life scratched out from the streets: skin the color of an overcast sky, dark circles under the eyes, crow's feet, and wrinkles appearing twenty years too early. A life filled with drugs, booze, cigarettes, and men who discarded them like old toys. She did not; she had a fresh clean look about her. Nobody would guess her profession. Most would imagine her as a soccer mom from the suburbs who worked nine-to-five in some innocuous corporate cubicle.

"Your last name DeRenzo?" I opened a bottle of a Cabernet and poured two glasses. I figured she would not object to smoothing off the edge a bit.

"You know? Of course you do. I never use my real name at work."

"Understandable. Plenty of times I should have used another name." She smiled, and I handed her a glass of wine.

"Thank you."

"Why didn't you call me?" I sat across from her.

"Too nervous. I heard how people can hack phones and listen to conversations."

"Why are you nervous? Has anyone threatened you?"

"No, but Kenzie was scared."

"Of what?"

"She wouldn't say." She hesitated, sipped her wine. "I pressed the issue, and she told me to stay out of it. Said I was better off not knowing anything."

"Was she protecting you?"

She shrugged.

"Who told you Kenzie was killed? Her name has not been released."

It was the only time she did not look at me when she spoke. Her eyes went down to the table for a second then back to me.

"A friend," she said.

"How did your friend find out?"

"Umm...not sure."

"And who's your friend?"

"Rather not say. She told me in confidence. You understand."

"She in the business?"

She nodded. Many years in the interrogation room taught me about eye contact when questioning a suspect. If they could not look me in the eye, it was a dead giveaway. Then there were the ones who would deliberately stare at me. In their mind, holding my gaze masked their guilt. Usually innocent ones would hold my eye in natural conversation, as Dee Dee did, except for the last few questions. Did the hooker network learn of Kenzie's murder and spread the word, or did she just make a mistake?

"When did you last talk to Kenzie?"

"We met for lunch three days ago. We always tried to meet at least once a week."

"Did she have a boyfriend?" I got up and grabbed a notebook and pen from the drawer.

"No."

"She talk about any guys?"

"Sure. But once they found out she was an escort, they would split. We had fun with it though. We would go to a bar, guys would talk to us, and we would make up different careers. One night we would be nurses, the next night we became lawyers." She threw her head back in a laugh. "The best one was when we told these two dudes we were in medical school to be gynecologists. They didn't know what to say. We had a great laugh because what we do and what a gynecologist does *do* involve the same body part."

We both laughed, then her tears fell. "I can't believe she's gone," she said. I gave her a few napkins to dry her eyes. "Please find her killer. I'll hire you."

"I understand you want answers, but the police are on it. Be patient, let them do their job."

"You and I both know it will go down as a hooker and a drug deal. Cops don't care. All due respect. If she was from some fancy rich suburb, they'd be all over it. Kenzie will only be a statistic in a few days."

"Not necessarily—"

"I can pay you, and I want the truth. She did not deserve to die the way she did. She was a good person. And my friend."

Neither of us said anything for a moment. She wiped her eyes.

"Stan already hired me. I'll do my best," I said.

"Thank you. I appreciate it."

She finished her wine and I offered a refill.

"No thanks. You are kind to hear me out. I should not have showed up like I did. I should go."

"I'm glad you did." We traded phone numbers and I called her a cab. "Anything else you can think of? Did she have any bad dates? Do drugs?"

"Nothing I can recall. And she was clean. Had been for years."

"You think of anything, call me."

"I will." She put her hand on my arm. "And we'll keep this meeting between us?"

"Of course."

We went downstairs and waited in the bar for the cab. After she left, I went back to my condo and poured another glass of wine. I liked Dee Dee but a feeling of uncertainty crept in. What did she know and when? Those were the questions she planted in my head. Did she come to me because she was scared, or was she paving the way to sneak a peek at my playbook without revealing hers?

13

The morning was cool and crisp, and I hit the ground running. Literally. An avid runner I was not, but sometimes I found an early run cleared my head and countered my inherent aversion to exercise. My usual route was to leave my condo and head toward the docks, loop around them for a mile or so, then back home. Not today, though. After fifteen minutes of a decent pace, I found myself in front of the Harbor Lofts building where Stan kept an apartment. Also, the spot where Kenzie Fitzgerald was thrown from the van.

I stood on the curb, not far from where Katie and I had parked that night. A few early morning delivery trucks rumbled by. The city coming to life for another day.

The way the young woman died bothered me. I never met her, but she was the catalyst to why Stan came to me. He said she threatened to blackmail him, but I'm not sure of anything at this point except that Kenzie was dead and Dee Dee was afraid. Most detectives would begin their investigation with the victim. Who were her associates, friends, and family? Life as a hooker placed her on the wrong side of the tracks. Then throw in stacks of cash and an abundance of drugs, the mixture becomes lethal in no time flat. Nobody should die the way she did, but the scumbags who killed her, they deserved to suffer. And part of me wanted to make that happen.

The question I did not ask Dee Dee was the one any decent detective would lead with: "Where were you when Kenzie was murdered?" Stan told me they were to meet at his love nest of a loft. Stan also panicked when he could not reach her by phone, later to learn she wasn't feeling well and took some cold medicine and fell asleep. She did not seem sick last night. Only scared. Why did my gut tell me I lacked the truth?

Did Dee Dee launch some sort of a pre-emptive strike by coming to my place last night? Was she afraid I would uncover something she wanted to keep covered? Did she want to ally with me, so I'd place her in the "good guy" column?

"Delarosa?"

A man's voice, but familiar. I turned around to find Paul Ellison behind me. "A little early for you, isn't it?"

"I can't do it," he said.

"What?"

"Run. I tried once. Bought new running shoes and gym shorts. The whole bit. Went to a high school and thought I would start by running around the track a few times. I made it about a hundred yards and couldn't decide if I should call an ambulance or an undertaker. Went home, showered, poured a drink, ordered a pizza, and gave my new workout gear to the first homeless guy I saw."

"Running is not for everyone."

"Not in the least."

"You could try walking."

He had a cup of coffee in his hand. "Perfect. I walked from the car to here."

"Why are you here?" I asked.

"Same reason you are. Working the case. Each new visit to the crime scene always reveals a new piece to the puzzle. As long as you let it."

"Ah, the stuff they don't teach in detective school."

"Yep. Stand still, observe, and listen. Let the scene fill your senses with information." He set his coffee cup on the curb, stood erect with his arms out, and closed his eyes. "Do not say a word. I need to concentrate and allow the spirit of Kenzie Fitzgerald to talk to me."

Oh, brother. "And what information is her spirit transmitting?"

"No talking. I can't concentrate if you distract me."

"If a patrol car drives by, I'm not saving your ass." I waited ten seconds. "How many have you had?"

"John? What do you take me for?"

"We worked in the same unit for eight years. I knew you better than your first two wives."

He opened his eyes and picked up his coffee. "Hey, the Irish say you can't drink all day if you don't start early. Plus, you broke my concentration by bringing up my ex-wives. Horrible, evil women. Why would you ruin my morning?"

"Yeah, my bad. You were the one drunk all the time and they were evil."

"It was because of them I drank."

"I'm leaving," I said. "Don't forget our deal."

"What? You don't want to know what the spirit of Kenzie told me?"

"That you shouldn't drink your breakfast?"

"Aw, I miss you, Johnny boy. That sense of humor."

He teetered on the curb while I stood with my arms folded and eyebrows raised.

"See the building right there?" He pointed to the Harbor Lofts. "Owned by one Stan Shelton. Remember him?"

"Of course. Football player, now owns car dealerships."

"You said your client is high profile and wanted to keep his name out of the papers."

I shrugged.

"We both know the girl was dumped on this spot. The first thing I did is see who owns the buildings in the area. And to my surprise, the Harbor Lofts is owned by a company controlled by Stan Shelton. So, I thought, was the old quarterback the target of the message? He doesn't exactly have a saintly past."

"What can I say?"

"I might be a drunk, my friend, but I'm still a damn smart detective."

"Best I ever worked with."

"Three days, John."

I watched him as he walked a half a block and got into his car. He drove off as sober as a nun on Sunday.

14

A plate of scrambled eggs, bacon, and toast appeared in front of me. My favorite breakfast in the best diner in town. When Nancy spots me coming through the door, my order goes in.

"Haven't seen you in a week or so. Been away?" Nancy said, as she refilled my coffee.

"Nah. Was doing some work out at my beach place. Came back two days ago when a new case came my way. Mike and Katie are on their way."

"Team meeting? I hope you are buying."

"Of course."

"Good, because I doubt you would open that musty wallet and spring for breakfast for the heck of it."

"Hey, I'm a good boss."

"And here you are in the cheapest place in town." She winked and went to another table. Nancy Carlisle and her husband Bill bought the diner, named it Nancy's, a year after he joined the Port City Police Department. She ran it during the week, and he helped on weekends. Ten years later cancer cut short their life together, leaving Nancy to run it by herself. It was her saving grace, though. It kept her busy while she worked through her grief.

After my unexpected meeting with Paul Ellison in front of the Harbor Lofts building, I ran back to my condo, showered, and sent a text message to Katie and Mike, inviting them to breakfast. Time to bring them up to speed and do some strategizing.

Mike arrived first and sat opposite. "What's up, partner?"

"Stan Shelton case."

"Yeah? Do tell."

"I'll wait for Blondie." I brought him current on what we discovered so far: Dee Dee, her brother Anthony, Kenzie, the warehouse of Entertainment Ventures, and the girl in the green Jag.

He shook his head. "I never liked Shelton. Loudmouth, king of the bullshit. You need to be careful jumping into his world. As a baseline, you probably only get half the truth with him at all times. He was a gambler and a cheat from the start. One of those guys always hustling somebody. Then he slaps his name on car dealerships. Perfect business for him. All hype and promotion."

"All this before your morning coffee."

Nancy came to the table. "Hi lover." She sat down next to Mike. "About time you came in. I'm stuck here dreaming about the day you sweep me off my feet and we run off together."

"Darling, I am almost there. Only need to save up a few more bucks, then off we go."

"Broken record with you. A girl can only wait so long." She stood and ran a hand through his hair. "You are going to miss your chance. I can only hold Johnny off for so long and he's wearing me down."

"Damn right," I said. "He who hesitates, loses. When you are knocking on the front door, I'll be taking her out the back."

"Sounds like you two have this all planned. I'm going to make my own breakfast." Mike started to stand, and she pushed him back down in his seat.

"You're my one and only. I got your breakfast," she said. The diner door opened, and Nancy whispered, "Your supermodel."

Katie sat down at the table. "It's nine o'clock in the morning," she said, with a killer scowl.

Mike and I were smart enough not to say a word. Nancy came with coffee and took orders.

"I don't know how you two drink your coffee black," Katie said, as she stirred cream and sugar in her cup.

I waited until she was done turning her coffee into some sort of latte. "I had a visitor last night after you left. Dee Dee."

"What? No way!" That woke her up.

"Surprised me in the alley. Wants to hire us to find Kenzie's killer. They were friends and she is scared and devastated by the murder."

"Stan told her he hired you to investigate the blackmail?" Mike asked.

"Yep."

He furrowed his brow and stared off in the distance. A familiar sign to me that his detective brain had latched on to an idea and shifted into high gear.

"Can't believe I missed her." Katie sat back in the chair and crossed her arms. "Then what?"

"She stayed for thirty minutes. We talked, I called her a cab, she left."

"Seriously? You are going to make me beg? I'm already in a crap mood because of a lack of sleep."

"You drove off and there she was. Hiding in the shadows. Startled me, too. If I had a gun on me, I might have shot her."

"She didn't want anyone to see her?" Katie fumbled in her purse for her notepad and pen.

"Right. Thinks she could be in danger and definitely didn't want Stan to know she wanted to hire me."

Katie jotted on her pad as she talked. "She wants to make sure Kenzie's killer is brought to justice and at the same time stay as far from the police as possible. So, she comes to us. If I was a hooker and my friend was killed, I would do the same thing. Did she add anything to what we know?"

Somehow, Katie's logic made sense. I nodded, and before I could offer my speculation on why Dee Dee came to see me, Mike tapped his knuckles on the table.

"Pre-emptive strike," he said. "She wants to distance herself from either Stan or Kenzie. My guess is she knows far more than she's willing to admit and yeah, I'm sure she is scared."

As usual, his instincts were dead on.

Nancy served both Mike and Katie a tall stack of pancakes with sausage links. She could eat as much as the big guy, and I had learned in the short time she was in my employ to not get between her and her food.

"One more thing," I said. "I ran into Paul Ellison in front of the Harbor Lofts building this morning. He already discovered Stan owns it. A matter of hours before he finds out Stan has an apartment there."

Katie's eyes went wide as she chewed.

Mike chuckled. "The master detective at work. Do not underestimate Ellison. He would absolutely devour a homicide case with a juicy celebrity like Shelton caught in the middle. A national headline case for sure, and a nice cap to Paul's career. He could stick it to the young bucks on his way out." Mike beamed.

Deep down, I knew he would love to watch the veteran detective score a huge win. I would, too. A victory for the old-school guys.

"We do what we can to help him get the collar," I said. Mike winked.

Katie was shoveling in pancakes, talking, and writing notes at the same time. Her phone chimed. "There's the police press release with Kenzie's name."

"They are just now releasing her name? Nothing last night?" I asked.

"I don't think—"

"So then—"

They both said it at the same time. "How did Dee Dee know it was Kenzie who was killed?"

I downed the last swallow of my coffee and grabbed a sausage off her plate. "Question of the day."

15

After breakfast we reconvened at McNally's where Mike and Katie prepared to open for the day. I parked myself in my booth and jotted some notes about the case. What began as an investigation into the attempted blackmail of Stan Shelton became a job with the goal of keeping Stan's neck out of a homicide noose. If the press got one whiff of the possible involvement of the ex-quarterback—albeit a lover of the spotlight—in a murder, they would hound him for the rest of his days.

The first order of business was to arrange a meeting with Dee Dee, so I tapped out a text message asking whether she could join me for lunch at noon, her choice of a location. She responded within a minute and suggested Max's, a downtown watering hole. It was a perfect place to meet. Dim lighting and a decent bar made it popular with city office workers. I had been there many times; it was on my beat when I worked Vice. I hoped we could tuck away in a back corner.

Katie and Mike were restocking beer at the bar when it began again, their voices loud enough to draw me from the booth.

"Were her kids home?" Katie poked.

He faced her as he set a case of beer on the bar. "No. I told you, she is not ready to tell her children about me. They are going through enough as it is with the divorce and all."

"Once again, that is my entire point. She will never tell them." Katie opened the case and loaded bottles into the cooler beneath the bar. "She wants you as her boy toy. A friend with benefits. Nothing more. Mike, all I'm saying is, I don't want you to get hurt when she moves on."

"Moves on? Why would she move on?"

I parked myself on a stool. No way did I want to miss this.

"All your dates are in her house when the kids are gone."

"So?"

"You don't think that is unusual?" she asked.

"Not under the circumstances. She's in the middle of a divorce. She can't be seen with another man until the divorce is final."

"Aren't they separated?"

"Yes, but she doesn't want to give the impression there was another man involved."

"Didn't they separate, like, a year ago?"

"Yes."

"And everyone knows her husband hooked up with another woman?"

"Yeah, his secretary."

"Then what is stopping the two of you from going out on a date?"

Mike set another case of beer on the bar. He folded his meaty arms on top of the box and leaned his large body against it. He paused. Then: "You think she has someone else, don't you?" he said, in a melancholy voice not typical of his gruff persona.

Katie stopped loading bottles, turned, and faced him. I was glad she picked up on his change in demeanor. "All I am saying is, I think it is weird you never go out. You only see her when it's convenient for her. Who knows if she has another 'friend'? Once she got separated, maybe she decided to play the field."

He shook his head. "She's not the type."

"I know you like her, but I love you, and I don't want your heart broken."

"She is not like that, you'll see—"

A knock on the front window stopped the conversation. We all turned. Paul Ellison peered in through the glass, his hands cupped around his face.

Mike looked at me. "Twice in one day?"

"All before noon. This ought to be interesting." I unlocked the door and let Paul in.

"I didn't know what time you opened," said the detective. "Thought I'd take a chance."

Mike reached out and shook his hand. "We open at eleven, but we're always open for you, Paul. Have a seat."

Ellison climbed on a stool and checked the time on his watch. "Eleven. I'll remember from now on." He wore the same rumpled brown suit and wrinkled white dress shirt he wore this morning and the day before. He did not wear a tie, and as I thought about it, I don't ever remember him wearing a tie.

"I can't believe yesterday was the first time I was in here," he said. "I got home last night and thought McNally's is the place for me to hang out. Old Mike and Johnny. Why didn't I think of this before?"

"Hey, you have your routine. Regular spots where they all know you. Why end a good thing?" Mike said, as he served him a shot of Jack Daniels and a beer chaser.

"Some of those places are getting a bit crowded. Too many people seeing me at all the wrong hours."

"We understand." I moved over and took the seat next to him. "Last thing you need is some rookie shocked to see you knock back a few during the day."

"Amen to that, Delarosa."

Mike poured two more shots and the three of us raised our glasses in a toast to old-fashioned police work—and to making it to retirement without being killed first.

Paul slid his glass to Mike for a refill and then looked at Katie. "What about you?" He patted the stool beside him. "I'm buying."

She smiled. "Thanks, but I'm on duty."

"Aren't we all, sweetheart."

"Some other time?"

"Sure. You'll be seeing a lot of me from now on."

She nodded and hurried off to the kitchen. Mostly, I'm sure, to remove herself from Paul's line of fire. He sat for another thirty minutes, drinking and reminiscing about the good old days as a cop in Port City, before getting up to leave.

"That's it for me, boys. Yes, my new home away from home." He threw a five-dollar bill on the bar, turned, and walked out.

It was amazing: he downed at least four shots in the short time he was there, and it had no effect on him. His organs must be so alcohol-logged that a few more drinks would not make a difference.

Mike held up the five.

"Professional courtesy," I said.

"The last thing Paul Ellison needs is another place to drink. He's keeping an eye on you and the case."

"Of course he is. Today was his way of making sure I keep my end of the deal. He smells a big score in Shelton. Hell, if he wraps up Stan in a murder, he goes out on a major high-profile arrest and retires like a king."

"Can't say I blame him."

"Me either. But I can't have him working against me. He and I need to be drinking from the same bottle."

Mike raised a shot glass. "Amen to that, Delarosa."

16

Paul Ellison's unexpected visit delayed me by thirty minutes for my lunch with Dee Dee. I sent her a text to ask if we could push it until 12:30. She agreed with an immediate return text. I wanted Katie to conduct surveillance, so I asked Mike whether I could steal her away from the bar for a bit.

"Nothing I can't handle. I do need her tonight, though."

"We'll be back mid-afternoon."

I had on jeans and a T-shirt which I didn't think appropriate for Max's, so I hurried to my condo and changed into khakis, a dress shirt, and a blazer. I grabbed my camera bag and met Katie at our garage in the alley behind the restaurant. We took my BMW and I had her drive. I thought the car would blend in better downtown at this hour than my old, vomit-brown Buick LeSabre, my go-to surveillance car.

When I first met with Stan, he gave me the phone number that Kenzie gave him. But when Kenzie was murdered, thoughts of calling the number vanished until today. I took a throw-away phone from the glove compartment and dialed.

"That's the number from Stan?" Katie asked.

I put the phone on speaker. "Don't expect anyone to answer." And nobody did. It only rang. "You can bet it's a burner."

"If it is, whoever has it might call back. They won't recognize your burner number. They might think Stan is calling."

"True. I like the way you think. So, we keep this phone with us in case." I pointed to a cross street on our left. "Turn here."

Max's was in the center of the block and the odds of finding a place to park that would give Katie an angle to take pictures were nil. We circled the block three times with no luck. It was now 12:25. She doubled-parked and I was about to get out and walk, when a delivery van pulled away from the curb across from the restaurant.

"There." We grabbed the spot and I hopped out, leaving her instructions to photograph anything and everything. Even a shot of her license plate would at least give us an address. All we had to work with was what Stan had told us. Dee Dee was still a mystery, and we needed to figure how to fit her into the puzzle.

The place was long and narrow, with a bar on the right and a dining room off to the left. People were two-deep at the bar. And here I thought we had our share of noon-time drinkers at McNally's. I snaked my way through the crowd to the rear of the place and grabbed a high-top table being vacated by two young women. I took the seat that gave me a view of the door.

A waitress came by and threw down a coaster.

"Bourbon with a little ice. Plus, a friend is joining me."

"Sure."

She hurried off and I scanned around the room. So far, no Dee Dee. I sent Katie a text:

"They have valet parking. Take pics of all cars."

She replied with a "thumbs-up" emoji. I took a sip of the whiskey and kept an eye on the door. Even though Dee Dee took me by surprise in the alley, and now had my suspicions on high, I did not press her for any information in our first meeting in my condo. She came to me asking for protection, so I wanted to gain her trust. My plan for this meeting was to dig deeper, but also make her feel confident that I could protect her while we figure out who eliminated Kenzie—and who orchestrated the blackmail scheme.

Fifteen minutes passed. No Dee Dee. No call or text.

I called Katie. "Anything?"

"No. But I don't know what she looks like. I take it she's late?"

"Yes, and I have one of those feelings."

"How long do we wait?"

"Until one, unless I hear from her."

"Copy that, boss."

I put the phone on the table and scanned the bar. All young professionals, most in business attire, but nobody resembling Dee Dee.

Five more minutes passed when the waitress came over and set another bourbon in front of me. "From the woman at the bar."

"Who?"

"Umm, she had on a tan ball cap. At the far end, close to the door. She asked what you were drinking. Guess you have an admirer."

I looked up and down the bar. I did not spot a woman with a tan cap, but a woman with long, black hair caught my eye as she was leaving. Her hair swished behind her as she went through the door. I threw down a twenty and called Katie while squeezing my way through the crowd.

"A tall woman with long, black hair—"

"I got her, I got her. Valet had a green Jaguar in front and she drove off."

I made it outside, but she had disappeared. I grabbed one of the valet guys. "A woman with long, black hair just got into a Jag. You know her?" I slipped him a ten.

He glanced at the money as he shook his head. "I wish."

"Ever see her before?"

"Nope. Why, you get rejected?"

"More like I got played."

17

"The waitress brought me a drink saying a woman at the bar sent it. A woman with a tan ball cap. I couldn't find anyone with a tan cap but did see a tall woman with black hair go out. That is when I called you."

"Definitely her. The woman from Entertainment Ventures yesterday. Green Jag and all. I took a lot of pictures."

Katie was still behind the wheel of my BMW, headed back to McNally's. I scrolled through the photos on the camera. "I agree, and it brings up many questions." I stopped on a picture of the valet kid holding the door open for the woman as she got into the Jaguar.

"Which means Dee Dee told her you were meeting there."

"Sure does. And sending me a drink was nothing more than a message—she knows who I am, and that she had eyes on me."

"A warning to stay off the case?" Katie asked.

"Yep. The question is, who is she?"

###

Katie and I no sooner walked into McNally's when my cell beeped with a message from Dee Dee:

"Very sorry about lunch. Something came up. A work thing.

Can I make it up to you? Buy you dinner tonight? Please?"

I handed her the phone and she read the text aloud as we explained to Mike what went down at Max's. "You're going to meet her, right? I'm going, too. Surveillance," she said.

"Yes, I am going, but you are staying here. First, Mike needs you, and second, we don't have a clue as to what is happening." I poured myself a bourbon and downed a healthy swallow. "If she is the same woman from yesterday, we can make the assumption that she is Dee Dee's boss with the escort service."

"We called her Pocahontas. She has long, black hair," added Katie.

"Wait," Mike said. "You said she wore a baseball cap?"

"The waitress told me a woman wearing a tan ball cap bought me a drink, and when it arrived, she knew I would immediately search the bar, so I figure she took it off so I wouldn't miss the hair as she left. She *wanted* me to see her."

Katie crossed her arms in front of her in a defiant stance. "Therefore, I need to go tonight. Surveillance and back up."

"No."

"Johnny, you can't go alone. I can stick a tracker on her car, take some pics."

"Too risky. I don't want Dee Dee or our mystery woman to know you exist."

"She probably saw me in the alley the other night, anyhow. And maybe Stan told her about me."

A rush of thoughts instantly shot through my mind. *What if Dee Dee was not here the other night to ask me for protection, but on some recon mission? Did our mystery woman send her? And how did Dee Dee learn it was Kenzie who was murdered before the police investigated?*

"I don't care. Stay out of sight. Not another word."

"It is server, by the way," she said.

"What?"

"You called the server a waitress. It's sexist."

I shot her a side eye glance that said, "not now," and poured another two fingers of bourbon in my glass. She huffed and went back to work. I retreated to the rear of the bar and leaned against the kitchen door. The non-meeting at Max's played over and over in my head. *What did I miss?*

Mike lumbered back. "Known you too long, partner. Something's got you twisted."

"The woman today. Sure as hell didn't catch her come in, which means she was in place before I got there."

"C'mon, Detective. This is an easy one." This was the Mike who became one of the best detectives to ever work the streets for the PCPD. He had an uncanny ability to imagine aspects to a case that other detectives could not. Inventing scenarios, even if far-fetched and unrealistic, would open his thinking and lead to new questions. He nailed this one immediately. "The woman, Pocahontas or whatever, she had help. Someone already inside who pointed you out. She buys the drink, then makes it easy for you to spot her as she leaves. Was the place crowded?"

"Packed."

"Works to her advantage. I say the first girl, Dee Dee, was there in disguise."

He ducked his large body through the door and into the kitchen. A moment later, he came out carrying a bucket of ice. "That's it, brother. Find out who this chick is. Key to the case, if you ask me."

Three young guys came in and took stools at the bar. They ordered drafts and asked Mike to put a European soccer game on the television. In behind them was a couple who wanted a table. Katie sat them and took their order. I stayed at the kitchen door and studied each person. Everyone appeared suspicious.

Who else worked for the tall, slim woman with the long, black hair?

18

The Shelton case file was spread out on my kitchen table. I grabbed a beer from the fridge and then sent a text to Dee Dee telling her to meet me at eight at Joey Mac's. She replied within a minute with a "yes" and a "thank you!" I gulped down half the beer, then called Stan.

He answered on the first ring in his best pitch-man voice. "Johnny, my good man, what can I do for you on this fine day?"

"You can meet me in one hour."

"Hold on a sec." He muffled the phone, but I heard voices and then a door closing. "Okay, I'm in my office. You have news on the girl? Was she my blackmailer? Johnny, I want this behind me. Haven't slept since all this happened."

"Can we talk in person?"

"Umm, yeah, sure, I can clear my schedule."

"There is a bar on the corner of Eighteenth and Chelsea. Joey Mac's. Park in the alley behind the building and use the back door."

"All sounds very cloak-and- dagger."

"Stan, one hour."

I hung up. I did not need to add the furtive element to the call, but I wanted him to heed the urgency. Two elements of this case did not jive for me. First, Stan's version of his relationship with Dee Dee—he believed she was more than an escort—was distinctly different from her take on their affair. If I was to keep his name out of the papers, I had to press him as much as possible. He hired me to find out who tried to blackmail him and so far, we had a dead escort and a determined detective who was quickly assembling pieces of the puzzle, and once he had it put together, it would make Stan front-page headlines.

Second, the woman who played me at Max's had me curious as hell. She identified me and made a show of proving it. Why? To tell me to back off? Or did she throw down a gauntlet to goad me to react?

The plan for the afternoon was now clear: to make Stan come clean about Dee Dee, and get the name of the tall slim woman with the long, black hair.

Traffic was light for mid-afternoon in the city and I pulled into the alley behind Joey Mac's thirty minutes ahead of Stan. The bar was in a residential neighborhood on the edge of Port City's Little Italy district.

The bald, gregarious Joe Maccarone almost dropped a glass when he spotted me coming through the rear entrance. He took the cigar from his mouth and held out his arms. "I'll be damned. The one and only Johnny Delarosa. And it's not even my birthday."

We hugged, and he had a boilermaker in front of me before I could sit on a stool. Joey Mac had fifteen years on the job when a gangbanger put two bullets in his lower back. He was beyond lucky—both shots barely missed his spine, but did enough damage to keep him from ever working the streets again. Three surgeries later, the PCPD offered him a choice: spend his last five years until retirement behind a desk or go out on disability. Joey on desk duty was unthinkable, so he made the exit with a permanent limp and within a year had managed to buy himself a business. It kept him busy; he got to hang out with his cop buddies and regale them with all his stories.

He took the stool beside me and immediately launched into one of his stories that I had suffered through so many times I could tell it myself. I held up a hand. "I'd love to reminisce but I'm on business. I need your help. Any guys around?"

One thing Joey loved more than talking was getting in on some action. "Are you shitting me? Hell yeah. Carmine is here. He's downstairs in the storeroom. What can we do?"

Carmine was Joey's son and also a former cop. Tall and muscular, unlike his short and round father, he retired at age forty-two after twenty years. He now ran his own security firm with a roster of cops who picked up extra cash working event security at parties and functions around the city. He also pitched in at the bar.

I checked my watch. "A client is meeting me here in twenty-five minutes. A high-profile type. But I need it to be quiet."

"Whatever you need, brother. Let me find Car."

"Joey, wait. What I'm asking might bend certain legalities. I don't want you guys jammed up."

"Damn, Delarosa. This is what I live for."

He limped off and was back with his son in less than a minute. We huddled at a table and I explained what I wanted. Their eyes went wide when I disclosed the name of my client. I also gave them a chance to back out, but they were sold.

"What about him?" I nodded to the only other person in the place. An older fellow with a long, gray ponytail. He nursed a bottle of beer and appeared to be lost in his own world.

"No worries," Joey said. "He's in here every day. I think he has old-timers. How'd you score this job, anyhow?"

"Are you shitting me, Joey? I'm the PI to the stars."

He laughed and pulled me to the front of the bar and pointed to a framed, autographed picture of Stan on the wall. "I met him right after he retired and moved to Port City. I loved him as a player and loved him even more after I learned he bet on games. My kind of guy."

"Play it cool, okay? Do your thing, though. He'll expect it."

"No problem."

We took our places and ten minutes later, Stan came in through the back, his body filling the doorway. He glanced around at all the sports memorabilia before joining me. "Johnny, why have I never been here? I love this place." He reached his long arm across the bar and shook Joey's hand. "Stan Shelton. You the owner?"

"Yes sir, Joe Maccarone. Welcome, Mr. Shelton. Been a fan since your college days."

"Call me Stan, please."

"Any chance I can get a picture?"

"You bet."

Joey hustled around and Stan threw an arm around him while I snapped a picture with my phone.

"It will go on the wall right next to that one." He pointed to Stan's photo.

"I'll make sure I come back and sign it. I love it here." As if someone flipped a switch, Stan began a random football story about a playoff game in Dallas.

Joey was enthralled, but I would be in for a long afternoon if I didn't break up their party.

"Stan, we have to talk. Football can wait." I took a seat at a table farthest from the bar.

"My fault," Joey said. "Stan, what are you drinking? On the house."

"Nope, I'm buying. Scotch, top shelf."

"Coming right up."

He continued to study the photos on the wall while waiting for his drink. He pointed to one of a famous pro baseball player from Port City. "He was incredible. Ever see him play, Johnny?"

I shook my head; frustration began to churn.

"Hey, I played with him, too." He tapped on a picture of a player who had been on the Jets. "He was a beast. So glad he played offense. Would hate to be tackled by him." Joey came back with the Scotch, set it on the table. "I met him before. A monster of a guy. Hell, I remember a time when he was in Baltimore and—"

"Stan." My tone said it all.

Joey disappeared to the back.

"Yes?"

"Sit down."

19

"Try again." I dealt the third hand of the same questions.

"Nothing else to tell, Johnny. On our first date, we ended up talking more than I ever talked to a woman. I mean, pouring my heart out. It was so natural and easy with her. Did you ever meet someone and experience an instant attraction? We clicked from the moment we met. Then it dawned on me. It was love at first sight. Something I never believed was real."

"We already established how you feel about her. I need you to tell me the things she did when you two were together. Outside the bedroom. Did she talk about anyone? Girlfriends? Old boyfriends? The job, her boss? Ever sneak out of the apartment and make a call? Anything of that sort."

"No, and I don't understand what you want." He swallowed back the last of his Scotch and got up from the table. "This is going nowhere."

"Wait. Sit back down." The scowl across his face displayed his frustration with my questioning, but instincts told me he might have information and not realize it. I needed him to think of everything and anything about their dates. "This is important, if you want me to help you." He took off his suit jacket and sat back down. "Another drink?"

"A short one. You got twenty minutes."

I waved to Joey for another round and started over. "You met her at random, right?"

"Yes, the website had pictures of the escorts and I selected her. She was the third or fourth girl I hired, and as I said, we hit it off from the start."

"Did she know you played football? Recognize you from the car commercials?"

"Yeah, on our second date together, she danced around the bedroom, saying she couldn't believe she was with a celebrity. Recognized me from TV. No clue of my life before the car business. When I told her of my sports career, it only made things better. The sex was incredible that night."

"Celebrity sex."

"Has some benefits."

"Let's move on. Did she ever tell you about her private life?"

"Not much."

"Ever mention any other job? Go to a gym? What about a social life?"

"She told me she worked out. I never really asked. She only wanted to discuss our future and all these fancy plans she had for our life together."

"She have any friends?"

"I remember one time she talked about going to a restaurant with a girlfriend. What's this got to do with the blackmail?" he said.

Joey brought more drinks. The door opened and two middle-aged men walked in. We were huddled at a table in the rear of the bar, but one of the guys immediately recognized the former quarterback.

"Johnny, Dee Dee would never—"

I held up a hand and stopped him as the man approached our table.

"Excuse me, sorry to interrupt. Are you Stan Shelton?"

"The last time I checked." He flashed his big toothy grin.

The man extended a hand. "Wow, I was a huge fan. I mean, I still am. Can I get an autograph?"

"Sure."

The chance meeting for the fan turned into an awkward moment when both realized neither had paper or a pen. Joey saved the day with a napkin and a marker. Stan turned on the charm and chatted with him for a minute about his favorite game. Favorite Shelton game, of course.

"Well, I'll be damned. Stan Shelton sitting in Joey Mac's." The man was all smiles as he walked away with his signed napkin.

"It has everything to do with the blackmail. And keep your voice down. The only way the blackmailer knew you hired escorts was through Dee Dee. Unless you told someone else about your hobby?"

"No, absolutely not."

"Think about the past few weeks. Where you went, people you were with. This is serious, brother. Somebody gave you up."

He stared into his drink. Swirled it around a few times. "Buddy of mine. I bragged about her and how amazing she was. But he would never say anything."

"What's his name?"

"Nope. You'll want to talk to him. The police will get wind. I can't bring my stupidity on him. And before you ask, yes, I trust him. He's the only one who stood by me way back when. In a time when nobody else wanted to be around me, he was there for me. So no, I will not serve him up."

In a crazy way, I respected his stand for his friend. I decided to ask the million-dollar question. "Do you know a Kendra Fitzgerald? Goes by Kenzie?"

He shook his head. "Who is she?"

"She was the blonde who was dumped in front of your building. Most likely it was her at the dealership."

His eyes popped wide. "You identified her? Damn."

"Police did."

He sat back in his chair. Stared at the ceiling for a minute, either for divine intervention or trying to figure out how much trouble he was in. He focused back on me. "They'll link her to me, won't they? They'll figure out I own the place."

"We are way past that. Kenzie Fitzgerald and Dee Dee used to be roommates."

His face went pale and expressionless. "What?"

"Did you know?"

He slowly shook his head. Either he was telling me the truth, or he had a great poker face.

"Dee Dee told me. She came to McNally's last night. Late. Said she was scared because she and Kenzie were friends and now, she's afraid. Wants me to find Kenzie's killer."

"She did? I can't believe this." He took a sip of Scotch, then another. Then finished it off in one gulp. "I'm screwed, aren't I?"

"Doomed maybe but answer this. How did Dee Dee find out it was Kenzie who was killed before the police released her name?"

All he could do was sit with his hands in his lap, his head tilted to the side and his eyes watery.

I thought it best to not speak for a bit. Let him chew on this the Shelton way.

"I described the girl to her. On the phone...from seeing her on the street."

"You said she didn't answer her phone all night. That's why you were so freaked out."

"Jesus, Johnny, I don't remember what I said...I...I left her a message, I suppose."

"All right. Go home, stay there. Do not say a word to anyone. No public appearances. You hired me to investigate the blackmail and keep you off the front page. I'll do what I can, but we only have a few days. Not going to lie—this will be a task, separating you from the escort agency and the dead girl. Cops probably have a list of questions by now." I was sure Paul Ellison had a few questions, maybe not a list, but this had to be a come-to-

Jesus moment for Stan. He needed to heed my instructions if I had any chance of bringing him through unscathed.

He pulled in a deep breath, then slowly let it out. I figured he was trying to calm a rising tide of anger or frustration or nerves. Or disappointment. "She would not betray me. We have a special bond. A trust," he said.

"Maybe you can regain the trust someday, but from this point forward—and this is your life lesson for today— do not trust anyone. Ever. Understand?"

He nodded.

"I'll call you. We will figure out where to meet."

"Whatever you say."

He got up from his seat, went to Joey and shook his hand. "My man, this joint is my new hangout. Quite a place you got here. Neighborhood bars are where the real people are. The blue-collar workers, the backbone of this country." Then he launched into a story about how he worked on a farm one summer while in high school.

He could not help himself. As if he didn't have a care in the world, the beloved, affable quarterback could not pass up a chance to endear himself to his public. It was in his wiring, his DNA, and deep in his soul. It made me realize at that moment, I could try to protect him from the thieves, the swindlers, and the blackmailers, but I would never be able to protect him from himself. After five minutes, I ushered him out the back.

Joey met me at the table with two shots of bourbon in his hand and we sat down.

"He looked like he saw a ghost. What did you do to him?" Joey asked.

"He did it to himself." We touched our glasses and threw back the whiskey. A minute later, Carmine came in.

"Any luck?" I asked.

"No problem," he said. "Blue Corvette, just like you said. Stuck the tracker in the right rear fender well. Got to admit, it was a bit of a rush. Reminded me of my old undercover days."

"Hold that thought. Security cameras in back?"

"Yeah, front, too."

"Any chance a couple of guys around tonight? No more than an hour. Pay in cash."

"Sure. Always one or two in here anyhow."

"Good, because today we have a doubleheader."

20

The meatball subs at Joey Mac's were world-renowned, at least in the ten square blocks of Port City's Little Italy. When he first opened, he had other sandwiches on the menu, but all anyone ever ordered was the meatball sub. The recipe was his mother's, so he named it Mama Maccarone's Meatball Masterpiece. Customers nicknamed it the 4-M. It was now the sole item on the menu, and he had just placed mine in front of me when my phone rang.

"Anything?"

"Yep, he left your location and went home for an hour. Then he drove to the Harbor Lofts building. Still there now."

"Thanks. Keep me posted."

Katie had let out a whoop and a holler when I told her we were successful in placing a tracker on Stan's car, forgiving me for not allowing her to go with me on the interview. Now she was involved in the action by watching his travels on her laptop, with instructions to text me when he was on the move.

I made short work of the meatball sub and washed it down with a draft beer. Dee Dee was scheduled at eight and part of me hoped the woman with the long, black hair would show up instead of her.

But at seven fifty-five, the door opened and in walked Dee Dee in jeans, flats, and a tight black T-shirt. I was at the same table from this afternoon, my back to the kitchen door and an unobstructed view of the entire bar. She saw me and smiled. I stood.

"Hi. I am so sorry about lunch today. Something I couldn't get out of."

"No problem." Instead of sitting opposite me she took the chair to my right.

"Isn't this the place with the famous meatball subs?" she asked, as she looked at all the sports memorabilia on the walls.

"Sure is. You want one?"

"No, no. Some other time. Wait, I was supposed to buy you dinner."

"Well," I said, "we have an excuse to come back."

She smiled an attractive and downright sexy smile and I saw why Stan lost his mind. She had an instant likeability about her. She was not nervous or scared the way she was the night before at my place. She was also somewhat upbeat considering her friend was murdered two nights before.

"How about a drink?" I asked.

"Wine. Red. The bolder the better."

"A woman of my own taste." I called Joey over and he came back with an eight-year-old Antinori Chianti Classico from Tuscany. I could not resist, so I canceled my bourbon, told him to leave the bottle and bring me a glass.

We toasted to meeting under more pleasant circumstances.

"So, here we are. Any developments in the case?" she asked.

"I wish I had something to tell you, but I don't. Kenzie's murder threw a curve into why Stan hired me. He told you of the blackmail attempt—at least, we assume it was to be an extortion of some sort. Did a job like that fit her character?"

She flashed a big smile. She slid her chair a few inches closer to me and placed her hand on mine.

Interesting.

She leaned in and whispered, "Let's not sugar coat it. We are hookers. Call girls. Whores. Money is the goal. Put enough cash in front of someone and they are capable of anything."

I nodded. "Truer words were never spoken. People do unimaginable acts for the promise of a payday. Kept me employed for all these years."

"Where are we then?"

"I have some questions."

"Ask away."

"How did you know Kenzie was killed before the police released her name?"

She removed her hand and leaned away from me a bit. "Umm...ah...let me think how the night went. I was home, in bed. I wasn't feeling well. I suffer from migraines every so often, so things were fuzzy, but Stan called me and said a girl was murdered outside his building. Thrown in the street. He described her—blonde hair, her clothes. I immediately thought of Kenzie. I was nervous from what I told you before. She was into something but would not tell me what. I could tell he was shaken and told him I would come over if he wanted. He told me no, said he had to leave. The night is a blur, and then I heard her name on the news today."

"Stan said he couldn't get you on the phone the night of Kenzie's murder."

She scrunched her brow. "Huh? I talked to him. His call woke me up."

Conflicting stories, but I decided to save the contradiction for later. "I'm sure he had it all mixed up," I said. "He definitely had a few that night, and you know how he gets when he's loaded."

"Oh, yes. Trips all over himself then passes out."

"He's out of his mind over you. Keeps talking about your future together. The feeling's mutual?"

She smiled and took another sip of wine. "In my business, I meet all sorts of men. With most, it stays all business. But somebody like Stan comes along, and you feel comfortable. Despite the public Stan we all see, he is different in private. He's not an arrogant jerk like many of them. He treats me well. He's generous, which is great. Yeah, I enjoy his company."

"He has deep feelings for you."

"And I don't want to hurt him in anyway. At first, he was into it for the sex. Then we started talking and over the next few dates a friendship sort of developed. He's genuinely a nice guy."

"But he's still only a client, right?"

"I quit high school in the eleventh grade, was turning tricks by nineteen. Danced in every club on the East Coast.

Spent all the money on drugs and alcohol. My thing was doing a line with a vodka chaser. Couldn't do enough. The bottom finally fell out after I did six months in some shit-hole jail in Florida. Came back to Port City and worked every crappy job you can think of. The turning point was when I got fired from a Dollar Store for getting high on my break. That same night, I ran into an old dancer friend and she told me she worked for an escort service and bragged about the money she was making. I cleaned up, kicked some habits, went to work for Fantasy. Three years later, I paid cash for my condo. So yeah, Stan is only a client. Besides, you think his wife would give him a divorce and leave all that cash? Hell no."

"So you keep playacting until his money stops?"

She leaned close and put her hand on mine again. Her eyes fixed on me. "What do you think?"

I glanced at her hand and was definitely picking up what she was laying down. "I can't afford you."

"I'm not on the clock."

"Personal relationships might be frowned upon."

"The owner has no problem with me and my personal life. Between my client roster and the money I bring in, if I was in sales I'd be salesperson of the year, with my own parking spot."

We laughed.

"I thought you were in sales," I said.

"Ha! Touché, Mr. Delarosa."

I refilled her glass. "Who is the owner?"

"Of the agency? Couldn't tell you."

"You don't know who you work for?"

"I guess some guy working in his basement who had enough brains to build a website. Everything is done online."

"You never interviewed with anyone when you were hired?"

"I met with a woman for about thirty minutes and she explained the process and said I could start. Gave me the name of a photographer to have pictures taken. Never said her name and I didn't ask. Every so often, an email pops up from someone named Miss T with information on my pay or something. Could be her."

"Is she local?"

"Not sure, but we've met a couple of times after that. Once she introduced me to a client in person. Another time we met for dinner. She told me I was the top earner in the company." She squeezed my forearm. "They tell me I'm talented."

"Definitely not shy."

"Life is too short. Go for it, I say. I find you very attractive and intriguing. Where do we go from here?"

"I'm not finished asking questions. And I don't sleep with clients." Her lower lip went out in a pout. I shook my head. "Bad idea. For now."

"For now?"

"Let's stick to the subject. Last night you were scared. Now you are...friendly and not worried at all."

"I freaked out last night and I'm embarrassed. I'm sorry. I woke up this morning realizing it has nothing to do with me. The cops question me, all I can tell them is what I told you."

"Absolutely. Stay away from Stan as much as you can until this blows over. If Kenzie was involved in some blackmail scam, it's probably over anyhow. And her murder, it is for the police to solve."

"Does this mean I am not a client anymore?" She flashed that sparkling smile and added a come-hither look.

"You are still a client. For now."

"Johnny, you are an interesting one." She finished her wine, picked up her phone and tapped an app. "Car service. Be here in a minute." She stood; we embraced, and she kissed me on the cheek. "Our paths will cross again."

Was that a threat or a warning?

"No doubt," I said.

She turned and walked out.

Joey came to the table. "Hubba hubba, Johnny. Touchy-feely type, huh?"

"With an agenda. She's the kind who will take all your money and you'll smile while she does it."

"I just want ten minutes."

"It will be your last ten minutes."

A moment later, Carmine came in. "Nothing, boss. She used a car service each way. Wish I had more for you."

I pulled some cash from my pocket and handed it to him. "No problem. Thank the guys for me."

"Hey, anytime. Keep me in mind."

I thanked Joey and headed out the back to my car. Sirens blared in my brain. Dee Dee had been taking money from men since she was nineteen years old, and she could teach a master class in it. All she needed was her smile, a wink, a whisper of flattery, and a soft caress. Too bad she never went to Hollywood; she gave and Oscar-worthy performance every night she's with a client. She'd work for Stan until his well ran dry.

She didn't want to sleep with me; she wanted to compromise me and get as much information on the case as she could. It was now my job to convince Stan he had to end it with her. Nothing good would to come of their arrangement.

21

No sooner did I walk into my condo, kick off my shoes, and stare into my empty fridge, than Katie called me.

"His car is moving and not toward his house. If I am reading the map right. I get mixed up on the maps."

"The Harbor Lofts building is downtown. Is he headed north? It would be toward where you live. What street is he on?"

"Umm...Logan. Heading south? Does that make sense?"

"Certainly not toward home. Keep watching."

"Where are you?"

"My condo, but now I am going to see what our friend is up to."

"Wait for me. Fifteen minutes."

I put her on speaker and opened my camera bag to make sure I had enough charge on the battery. "No, I'm leaving now. Where is he?"

"Turned...oh my God, Johnny...he turned onto Commons. That's where Entertainment Ventures is."

"On my way."

###

Commons Boulevard was less than ten minutes from my place at this time of night. I stopped a half-block from the entrance to the business park, twisted the 300-mm lens on the camera, and walked until I had a view of the building. Sure enough, Stan's blue Corvette was parked next to the green Jaguar. Both in front of the office door. An expanse of lawn with a few trees was between the road and the complex, and enough cars in the lot to hopefully give me a concealed vantage point. Not sure what I was going to photograph, unless I got a clear shot of the woman with the long, black hair. I wondered whether she was the one Dee Dee mentioned—Miss T.

I made my way across the grassy area, going from tree to tree. Office lights were on at both Entertainment Ventures and Amazing Graphics, the T-shirt design business to the left. Gary's Auto Body, to the right, was dark. I found a spot behind a delivery van the graphics shop had parked on the opposite side of the lot. It gave me a clear line of sight of the cars and the door.

My phone vibrated; it was a text from Katie asking for an update. On the drive over, I told her text only, no calls. I responded, telling her the car was here and I was going to wait.

I sat on the curb with my legs extended under the van and my arms leaning on the right corner of the van's rear bumper. With the long lens, and the light from two streetlights in the parking lot, I had a decent shot when they came out.

Ten minutes crept by. I thought for sure it was an hour. There was nothing worse than surveillance when there was nothing to do but watch and wait. Another fifteen had elapsed when two young guys came out of the graphics shop. One leaned against the building and lit a cigarette while the other started across the lot toward the van. If he came around the back, I was screwed. If he got in and drove off, I was screwed. I pulled the camera to my lap and moved more to the center of the bumper. It occurred to me I didn't have a weapon. Not that I needed one, but it could be helpful when explaining my way out of a situation. I doubted the two workers were packing.

The worker opened the van's side door, rummaged around a bit then slammed it closed.

"I found it," he shouted.

I moved back to the right corner. The T-shirt guys were passing a pint bottle of liquor back and forth. Their break ended and I wondered about the quality of the work coming from those two after finishing off the whiskey.

Every fifteen minutes, Katie checked in with a text. I reported the same: nothing. Thoughts of abandoning my post and making my way to the rear of the building and the loading dock began to form. I wondered whether I was missing something around back. But if I moved now, I ran the risk of not seeing anyone come out the front.

The choice was made for me. The door opened and out walked two people, the woman with the long, black hair, and Dee Dee. *Well, I'll be damned.* Maybe this woman was Miss T after all and Dee Dee met with her more than we thought. It also meant she went to Stan's love loft and borrowed his car. I did snap a nice close shot of the mystery woman. They chatted for a few seconds before driving off in their respective cars.

"Police. Do not move. Put the camera down and your hands in the air."

A woman's voice behind me. My heart pounded; she scared the hell out of me.

"Stand up."

I raised my hands. "Easy now. I'm on the job." My phone vibrated in my pocket. I pulled my legs back from under the van and stood.

"Hands against the van. Spread your legs." I complied and she did a quick frisk. "Turn around, slowly. Keep your hands where I can see them."

I did. A Glock was aimed at my face, held by a female dressed in all black—shoes, leggings, pullover, and ski cap. Relief and shock hit simultaneously. An all-too-familiar face.

"Monica?"

She took a step closer. "Delarosa? What the hell?"

"I guess I could ask you the same thing." My phone vibrated again.

"That your phone? And put your hands down."

"My office calling."

She holstered the pistol. "You have an office?"

"Sort of."

She stuck her hands on her hips. "Well, I'll be damned. Johnny Delarosa." Her head bobbed; her eyes went over me. "Been a while. You're not fat and bald."

"You look good too, Mad Dog."

"I can't wait to find out why you are out here."

"Maybe we should catch up."

"Still a bourbon man?"

"Thought you'd never ask."

22

"Are you kidding me?" Mike almost dropped the tray of beer mugs in his hands. Monica and I came in the rear door of McNally's as he entered the kitchen. "Where did you find her?" He set the tray on a counter and wrapped his beefy arms around her.

"You big red-haired giant. How the hell are you?" She stepped back to size him up. "How long has it been?"

"Too long. Talk about a surprise. You want to tell me what's happening?"

"Over some whiskey—top shelf, too," I said, and brought Monica in from the kitchen and told her the history of how Mike and I continued our partnership into the bar business. He shooed out one last barfly and locked the door. We settled in my booth with a bottle of Woodford Reserve bourbon and three glasses.

Monica Mattson became a detective about the same time I did but was assigned to Vice from the start. The word on her was that she was an intuitive and thorough detective, but that she did not play well with others. Too independent, had to do things her way. She had a uniqueness to her, both in her physical appearance and in her demeanor. She was a very light-skinned African American, with freckles. She had an undeniable cuteness, and a cool sexiness about her that she tried to downplay but couldn't. She never dated other officers and after many guys asked and failed, the only reasonable explanation they could concoct was that she must be a lesbian. She dispelled that rumor when she made a rare appearance at a Christmas party with a man whom she introduced as her boyfriend.

She was different, and that made her a target of the ribbing, trash talk, the insults cops need to stay sane, and the downright vulgar, blatant sexual harassment from weak men who had a masochistic streak they used to convince themselves they were men. They never stopped and she did her best to ignore them, using exercise as an outlet. She was obsessed, in the gym at least five days a week, going through the most intense workouts I ever witnessed. I always thought it was her way of blowing off the rage that welled in her, fueled by the constant barrage of idiocy directed her way.

The harassment, trash talk, and rage all came to a head one morning in the squad room, when a detective named Dunston—they called him "the Dunce" for short because he was dumb, obnoxious, vulgar, and annoying—proved his nickname when he decided to poke the bear. He had a habit of calling her M&Ms, and on that particular morning, he took a fateful step over the line. "Hey, Mattson, you say you are chocolate on the inside but have that light candy coating on the outside. When we have sex, does that mean you'll melt in my mouth instead of my hand?" He chuckled, all proud of his joke. A few other guys laughed too, but the rest of us knew what hell was headed his way.

In one swift motion, she slammed him against the lockers with her right hand in a vise grip around his throat and her left hand squeezing the life out of his balls. She had him pinned, his face blood red and about to explode; his arms swung in feeble attempts to knock her off. He choked, squealed, and begged while she let go with a string of obscenities so vile it would make a drunken sailor cringe. Finally, two officers, who delighted in Dunce's beat down, reluctantly pulled her off. He fell to the floor with both hands on his crotch and whimpering like a baby.

Mattson, as if nothing happened, stood with her hands on her hips and scanned the room. "Anyone else want a piece of candy?" From that moment forward, she earned the respect of every officer in the department and was bestowed with the moniker Mad Dog.

Luckily for me, she and I always had a cool rapport. We both respected our mutual proclivity for bending the rules. I hadn't seen her since I retired over six years ago.

We toasted to the good old days.

"Been a while, boys. I heard you two had a place, but you know me, not much of a social type."

"No excuse," said Mike. "You look fantastic, Mad Dog. Keeping yourself in shape."

"Finished my third Iron Man triathlon last month."

"Wow, impressive. I'm out of breath carrying kegs in and out of the bar." He grabbed her left hand. "No ring, huh?"

"Mike, c'mon. Nothing's changed with me. No time for relationship bullshit. You guys?"

"Both divorced. We learned the hard way," I said.

"See, that's what I'm talking about."

She had removed the ski cap when she came in and her black hair was straight and pulled back in a ponytail. She had to be mid-forties by now and had not aged a bit. She was lean and fit, and still had the freckle-cuteness turned up high. Not a line on her face, and her dark eyes had the sparkle I remembered.

"Not to ruin our reunion, but we have business at hand," I said. "You go first."

"Nah, I'm the police, don't forget. You need to show me yours before you see any of my goodies."

We all laughed, and Mike poured more Woodford in our glasses. "Monica, you always had that wall up. You and I would have been amazing together."

"Very few ever make it over the wall. Don't even think about it."

Mike hung his head.

"C'mon, Johnny, spill the beans. And don't hold back. We had that same whatever-it-takes attitude to serve up justice. I hope it has not changed."

"Never. This stays here for now."

"Deal."

"My client hires escorts from Fantasy Escorts—"

"Owned by Entertainment Ventures."

"Yes, and he is a bit of a celebrity. Somebody found out, called him and alluded to a blackmail attempt."

"And?"

"We suspect the young woman who was murdered and thrown out of a van in front of the Harbor Lofts building the other night was the one attempting the extortion."

"Sounds like your client is guilty."

I shook my head. "I was there when it happened."

"At the Lofts building? Maybe you better start over. From the top."

I explained everything, including the odd meeting with Dee Dee earlier in the evening, the non-lunch at Max's, the mystery woman with the long, black hair, and how the extortion attempt might be over. I said everything except Stan's name.

"That was Dee Dee driving the blue Corvette tonight?"

"Yep."

"The car that just happens to be registered to Stan Shelton. The former quarterback, and now owner of six car dealerships in the city. He's a bit of a celebrity."

"You ran the tags." I raised my glass to her. "Your turn. Show your goodies."

"Wait, did you follow Dee Dee tonight after you met with her?"

"No. Well, sort of."

It only took her a few seconds. "You hacked the car's GPS?"

"Not exactly. She used a car service from Joey Mac's, then borrowed Stan's car."

"You thought you were following Stan?"

"Umm, no."

"You best not tell me you have a tracker on his car."

I smiled. "Prefer to call it Mad Dog style."

"Funny, but I wish. You're lucky I like you two. Keep talking."

"My questions are, who is the woman with the long hair, and just how involved is Dee Dee? She told me she never meets with the owner, then shows up at the office tonight. Who is my mystery woman?"

She stretched her arms above her head. "Getting late. This unexpected reunion was great, and I do love you guys, but I have an early morning."

"No way, Monica. Your turn."

"Okay, okay. Three months ago, we got a call from NYPD about a sex trafficking operation. They were working it but told us the girls were coming in through Port City. Captain put me on it, and it has been my only case since. The information New York gave us eventually led to Entertainment Ventures and the woman with the black hair. But it's as if she doesn't exist. Everything is wrapped up in layer upon layer of LLCs and corporate holdings. One company is the parent company of the next, and so on. If she is the mastermind, she's one damn smart woman."

"The woman, what's her name? Give me that, then come back tomorrow when the real detective is here."

"I followed her into a hair salon and sweet-talked the girl at the front desk. Talia Thorne. Probably fake. You won't find anything. No driver's license, tax returns, nothing. Lives in an apartment downtown leased to Entertainment Ventures."

"Why not bring her in?" Mike asked, before I could.

"From what we understand, the trafficking is huge. Can't risk tipping her off."

"Wow. Never thought this case would go in that direction," I said. "Makes me wonder if Stan is involved?"

"I doubt it, but we need to compare notes. Your new friend Dee Dee is all new to me."

"You need to be concerned about Paul Ellison. He's the lead on the girl's murder and he already sniffed out Stan."

"Ellison?" Her eyebrows went up in surprise.

"You know him?"

"Only by reputation and it's not flattering."

"No matter what you heard, he's a damn good detective. His question being, 'who killed the girl.' And if his investigation leads to the trafficking, your case is jacked. Be here at eleven tomorrow morning. We're his first stop."

"Serious?"

"Eleven."

"If nothing else, it will be worth the entertainment value," Mike said. "I can't wait for his reaction when he meets you."

"Is he going to be a problem?"

"To be determined," I said.

She finished her drink, got out of the booth, and we all exchanged hugs. I walked her out to the alley and to her black Camaro, which fit her persona perfectly: sleek, black, and tough.

Back inside, I cleaned the bar while Mike swept and mopped the floor.

"Johnny, my gut tells me Shelton has nothing to do with Mad Dog's case. You can try to keep his name clean, but this trafficking stuff is way out of our league. If he has himself mixed up in that, God help him."

"I agree, but the whole Dee Dee thing was too weird. Last night she was scared, tonight she was in a good mood and way too friendly."

"Yeah?"

"Not even subtle. Odd, really. Oh, and totally playing Stan. He's in love, but to her, he is another fish on the line."

We locked up the bar for the night and both agreed the morning should be quite interesting.

I was too wired to sleep. Too many parts of today played over in my mind. The strange lunch at Max's, the weird meeting with Dee Dee, her using Stan's car, and running into Monica after all these years. I took my camera out to the balcony and stretched out on my chaise lounge to scroll through the pictures from earlier. I stopped on the picture of the woman with the long, black hair. Talia Thorne. I zoomed in on her face. Stared at it, studied it. *Familiar. Seen it before.*

I laid the chair back and closed my eyes. I needed my brain to shut off for the night, but it was not going to happen. Images flashed by, from today, yesterday. Stan. Katie singing the Shelton jingle. Kenzie in the street. Dee

Dee with her hand on mine. The woman with the long, black hair.

The woman with the long, black hair. I bolted from the chaise and hurried to the walk-in closet in my bedroom. I pulled down from the top shelf a shoebox I used to hold my mementos. I opened it. My pocketknife from Boy Scouts, my first Communion pin, the badge the PCPD gave me when I retired, and the note.

The note from a little girl I knew for three days many years ago. I gently removed it from the envelope and unfolded it.

Johnny. Thank you. I love you.

I stared at the paper.

It couldn't be.

23

The revelation that Talia Thorne could be the young girl I harbored for three days twenty years ago consumed me. Every thought was about her. Did she also have the same revelation when she learned Stan hired me? Did her memory flash to the time she spent with me and that's why she pulled the strange lunch greeting at Max's? So she could take a look at me and confirm I was the police officer who befriended her? Or, did she already know and wanted me to have a glimpse of her? Nevertheless, I would not rest until we met and with any luck, we'd both find the answers we sought.

No matter what my mind was churning, it was morning and I had a business to open. Paul Ellison had his face pressed to the front window when I came down from my condo at ten to begin the set up for the day. Mike usually rolled in at ten thirty; Katie arrived by eleven.

I unlocked the door for him. "Early, aren't you?"

"Johnny boy, what a fine morning. Did you run?"

"Not today. Had a bit of a late night."

He settled on a stool and I put a glass and a fifth of Jack Daniels in front of him. He poured a man-sized breakfast portion. Most people needed coffee in the morning; he needed Tennessee whiskey. I first checked the taps and then began to cut lemons and limes while he watched. "You want to take over here? Earn your spot at the bar."

"Nah, I'm much better from this side. What you got for me? Anything new?"

"I want you to meet somebody. In a few minutes." I nodded toward the bottle. "Go slow."

"Delarosa. No surprises."

"You'll be fine."

"Remember, I can expose your friend in a matter of seconds."

"Who?"

"The one who can put me in a new Chevrolet."

I stopped cutting lemons and aimed the knife at him. "He was set up to be the victim. My job is to keep him out of the papers. I'm asking you don't look his way until you are left with no choice."

"But all it takes is one reporter to discover Shelton owned the building. The first story will be," he held his hands up, making air quotes, "'what a coincidence. The famed football star owns the building where the girl was murdered.' But if the same reporter gets a whiff of anything shady, Shelton will be the first name you read."

"And cops who leak stories to the press don't stay cops very long."

"Just saying."

"I'm telling you, we work together. Quid pro quo."

"I don't speak Spanish."

"Uh huh."

The ice hopper under the bar was empty, so I filled two buckets in the kitchen. I was on my way back when I stopped at the door and stood, observing Paul. He had the glass in his left hand and the bottle in his right. He would drink nonstop. Pour refill after refill. There was no tasting the whiskey, enjoying it. He needed to down as much as he could to function. A pang of sympathy went through me and I realized how much the alcohol controlled him. Like most alcoholics, I guess. He'd be one of those guys who retires and dies six months later, leaving a whole lot of life on the table. Or the bar, in his case.

Katie came in. "A black Camaro is in my parking spot."

I moved the whiskey away from Paul and poured him a ginger ale.

"Hey, what the hell are you doing?"

"Protecting you. Sit tight."

Katie grabbed my arm. "It has tinted windows. Couldn't see if anyone was inside."

"I'll fill you in. A lot to tell from last night." Out of the corner of my eye, I caught Paul dumping a shot of whiskey into the ginger ale. "Ellison, stop. Trust me." I stashed the bottle on a shelf.

Monica came in through the back. Dressed in all black again, but now a business suit of slacks, blouse, and a blazer. She was a head-turner no matter what she wore.

Paul recognized her. "Is that who I think it is?"

She was headed our way and Katie said, "Who is she?"

Monica extended a hand to Ellison. "Monica Mattson. Pleasure to meet you, Detective."

"You, too. I always wanted to meet you, but our paths never seemed to cross. Your reputation proceeds you."

"Uh huh. Yours, too." She said to me, "The booth?"

I nodded.

Katie held up her hands and mouthed, "Who is it?"

Paul slid into the booth across from me, and Monica sat next to him.

She wasted no time. "Detective, Kenzie Fitzgerald worked for a company I am investigating."

"The escort service?"

"Entertainment Ventures."

"What kind of case? I can help."

"Nope. What you can do is stay in your lane. Investigate the murder, period. You come across anything that seems off or doesn't fit, or something you think might help me, you call." She slid him her business card.

"Hold up. First, I don't appreciate your tone, and second, I'm the senior detective. How about we start with your case?"

Monica shifted around to face him, and I thought it prudent to interrupt. "Monica, give him something. You two might make more progress if you play nice."

She considered for a minute and I was sure she was calculating on what to say to him without giving up too much. "We were contacted a few months ago by NYPD about a sex trafficking ring that could be running girls through Port City on their way to New York. Entertainment Ventures has come up in the investigation. Not much else to tell. You see or hear anything odd that could relate, tell me."

"Damn, Mattson. Yeah, no problem. But it's a two-way street. I have a murder to solve, so if you dig up anything—"

Katie slid into the booth next to me, across from Monica, with her pen and notepad. She held out her hand. "Hi, I'm Katie." It was horrible timing, but it probably saved Ellison from a verbal dress down.

Monica ignored her hand, looked her over. "Oh, no thanks. Nothing for me."

"Monica, this is Katie Pitts. She works for me. Research."

"And I'm an apprentice private investigator," Katie chirped.

Ellison took a large gulp of his laced ginger ale, sat back and folded his arms, as if he couldn't wait for this show to begin.

I think it blew Monica's mind that this girl interrupted her. "I thought you were Waitress Barbie here to take our order."

The comment took Katie aback. She stiffened in her seat. "No, sorry. I'm taking notes."

Monica stared at her, as if the female lion were sizing up her prey, deciding when to pounce and eat her alive. Katie only smiled and squirmed.

Monica turned back to Ellison. "Stay in your lane, and yeah, we keep each other updated. One other thing—I know you are close to retirement, and you would love to go out with a bang, but I'll put you out to pasture right now if you screw up my case. Understood?"

"Yes, ma'am."

She got up to allow him out.

He mouthed, "Good luck," to me as he left.

Before Monica could get back into the booth, Mike slipped in. "What did I miss?"

"You missed Ellison get his orders," I said.

"Take it easy on the old guy. He's killing time until he can submit his papers."

"Hey, last thing I need is that old drunk in my way." She propped her elbows on the table and set her sights back on Katie. "You enjoy the PI work?"

"I love it. Johnny's been teaching me; I mean whenever I can go in the field with him. But the research part is fun, too. I can't believe the things you can find out about people. My favorite is surveillance, but not really because it can be long and boring, but also exciting at the same time. I'm sure you already know all this. What weapon do you carry? I've been wanting a concealed carry permit, but he won't allow me yet. I need to learn to shoot, first." She cocked an eyebrow. "Right, Johnny?"

"We are taking it one step at a time." My face got hot. Out of the corner of my eye, I saw Mike bite his lip.

"What do you pack, Detective?" Katie asked.

"Well, I *carry* a Glock 9mm." She pulled it from her shoulder holster under her jacket and laid it on the table. Then she stood and put one foot on the bench and raised her pant leg. "And this little guy." She put a small gun beside the Glock. "A 45-caliber Derringer." She reached around her back and produced a third weapon. "A Beretta 9mm. Just in case."

Katie's eyes were wide and so were mine. "Wow. Impressive."

"I'll train you to shoot, if you want. These guys will teach you one way—I'll show you the correct way."

"Serious?"

"Anytime. When we finish this business."

"Yes, def. Johnny, is that okay?"

"Absolutely. Detective Mattson is the best in the business. Hey, would you mind making some drinks?"

"No, not at all." She left with our order: the usual for me and Mike, a soda for Monica.

"Mad Dog, what are you doing?" I asked.

"I like her. Yeah, she's young and naïve, but for some reason, I'll help her. Reminds me of myself."

"What? You two can't be more different."

"How do you know? Might surprise you what you don't know about me. But I will tell you this—if I find out either of you are banging her, I'll kill you."

Mike threw up his hands. "There's the Mad Dog we love. Now I'm better. You had me worried there for a minute."

Monica's phone rang and she excused herself from the table just as Katie came back with the drinks.

"She is so cool. You guys worked with her?"

"Yep, we each did. One tough chick, though. Did everything with incredible intensity, one hundred and ten percent all the time. Nobody carries three guns."

Monica came back. "Katie, I have an assignment for you." She wrote some notes on Katie's pad. "Two trucking companies. Pull everything you can. Drivers, routes, what they're hauling, anything." She handed her a business card. "Call me when you have something."

"You got it. Thanks. I'll start right away. I'm really looking forward to working with you. I think we have a synergy—"

"Stop talking. Do a good job here and if you want, I'll teach you things these two Neanderthals cannot. I'll train you, and if you work hard, you'll be the strongest, meanest, most bitchin' badass in the city. It's up to you. I got to go. Johnny, I will call you later. I need your help."

Mad Dog went out through the back. Mike and I both turned to Katie.

She had Monica's business card in her hand and looked at us with those gorgeous baby blues. She was in awe. "I love her."

24

Once the lunch crowd began to dissipate, I went upstairs to my condo and fired off a text to Dee Dee asking whether she could arrange a meeting with Miss T. I emphasized it was strictly routine, and that I only wanted to ask a few questions. She sent an, "I'll see what I can do" response. We had to meet, no question, and I knew in my gut that she wanted the same. Why else would she want a peek at me at Max's?

How could this all be a coincidence? Stan coming to me with the blackmail scheme only to learn the woman who owns Entertainment Ventures might be the girl I took off the streets in a valiant, but failed, attempt to rescue her? It was beyond bizarre, but I had seen things in my twenty-six-year career that I never thought possible.

Mike called. "Is Katie up there with you?"

"No, why?"

"She said she had an errand to run, but she's been gone for forty-five minutes. I have three tables and a bunch of guys at the bar."

"On my way."

The note from the sixteen-year-old Talia Thorne—of course she never told me her name, and I still did not know whether it really was her—was on my table. I carefully folded it and placed it back in the shoebox, then tucked the box back in place in the closet.

I jumped in behind the bar while Mike took care of the tables and handled food orders. Katie disappearing for almost an hour was not her style. The Shelton case and now my past coming back to confront me in the form of Talia Thorne was disconcerting. Too many unknowns and variables for her to be gone without telling either of us what she was doing. She was eager to please, but her inexperience and naivete could quickly get her in trouble. I hoped she did not decide to investigate a lead on her own.

My phone rang. Katie? No, it was Stan's name on the screen.

"Johnny, I got another call. The same man who called me the first time. He said this is not over, and time is short."

"What did you say?"

"That I was with some people and couldn't talk. Which was the truth. He is giving me one hour and calling back."

"Where are you?"

"Dealership. In my office."

"Can you be at Joey Mac's in thirty minutes?"

"Yes."

"Park in the alley. Don't talk to anyone."

I pulled Mike aside. "Shelton received another call. I'm meeting him at Joey's. Sorry to leave."

"They make a demand?"

"Somehow he bought an hour. I need to stop him before he does something stupid."

"Yeah, go. Hopefully, she—"

Something caught his eye. Katie. Mike and I—and the eight other guys in the place—could only stare.

She was dressed in skintight, black everything: jeans, low-cut T-shirt, motorcycle boots, and a leather jacket, which she put on as she walked up to us. She had her hair pulled back and black sunglasses parked on her head.

"What? No time like the present to begin my new life. I'll handle drinks."

The guys at the tables all moved to the bar.

"Monica created a monster," I said.

"Bright side, brother. She'll be great for business."

Joey Mac intercepted me as I walked in. "Johnny, what's going on? He's been here for fifteen minutes and damn, that boy can talk. I thought I ran my mouth, but holy shit, I couldn't break away from him, and I have orders stacking up."

"Sorry. Thanks."

Stan was at a table with a draft beer in front of him, and jumped up and threw a bear hug around me. "What do we do?"

"We wait for the call. Did he say anything about a demand?"

"No, nothing."

We moved to Stan's Corvette in the alley. There must be a medication available for people like Stan. He would go from panicked about the fear of being caught up in a scandal, to telling one of his tall tales of a fantastic finish of a football game, or one of his stories of meeting some amazing woman at a party, or how he used to trade his game jerseys for sex when in college, and then back to being in a panic about the extortion. I'm not sure I said three words in the entire thirty minutes.

The call came exactly one hour from the first contact. He pressed the phone's speaker for me to listen in, and I had a notepad to use to coach him. I jotted down the phone number. He answered.

"Smart of you to answer," the voice said.

"What do you want?"

"We want what you agreed on."

"And if I don't?"

"Don't be stupid. Stick to the deal. I just sent you a routing number and bank account. Twenty-four hours to make the transfer." The call ended.

His phone beeped with a text of the bank information which I wrote on my pad.

"Johnny, what do I do?"

"What's the agreement?"

"If I don't pay, they are going to go public about me hiring girls."

"He said stick to the deal. Did you make a deal with these people?"

"No, of course not. I'm being blackmailed, isn't it obvious?" Beads of sweat appeared on his forehead, and he yanked at his tie and opened his shirt collar.

"No, he never said an amount. Did you forget to tell me something? How much do they want, and when did they tell you?"

"I told you, one million. The girl told me at the dealership."

"You never told me. Stan, you need to come clean with me or I'm done."

"This whole business has me so upset I don't know what I'm saying. I'm confused about everything. You got to help me. If I didn't tell you about the money, I forgot. I'm sorry. Can you blame me, though? How do I get out of this without Nikki finding out?"

"Maybe you don't."

His face was red, and his eyes teared up.

"You either pay, or we go to the police and fess up. Allow them to intervene," I said.

"Out of the question. I can't transfer that much cash without Nikki's approval. We go to the cops, my name will be in the paper tomorrow." He stopped, stared out of his window for a minute. "You talk to them. That's what I want. Tell them I don't have that kind of money. If anyone can do it, you can. Please talk to them for me."

My cell buzzed. I held it to make sure Stan could not see it was a text from Dee Dee.

"She'll meet with you tonight. Details in a bit."

I slipped the phone into my pocket and sat in silence for a moment.

"What else do I need to know?" I asked.

"Nothing, I swear. Johnny, thank you."

"If you are holding anything back and sending me in blind, I guarantee your name will be the front-page headline on every paper in the country. Do you understand?"

"Yeah, sure, Johnny, sure."

"Go home. Stay there until I call you."

"Will do. I promise."

I got out of his car and watched as he drove off. If this went sideways because he wasn't telling me everything, I'd hit him so hard it would make a sack from a three-hundred-pound lineman feel like a kiss on the cheek.

25

The meeting I requested with Miss T—or Talia Thorne, I presume—was set for eleven that night. The instructions for Katie were simple: to work from my condo and monitor the GPS we permanently kept on my car. If I did not contact her within two hours, call Monica Mattson and tell her about the meeting. I also had her monitor the tracker Carmine hid on Stan's car, just in case, and to make sure he stayed put in his home.

I sent Monica the bank account numbers given to Stan on the phone call. She reported back in less than an hour that the bank was located on Grand Cayman Island and because of the strict banking laws, it would be next to impossible to gain any information on the account owners. It also told me they had some smarts about them.

I made sure my phone was fully charged and my Beretta loaded. I pulled a blazer on over the shoulder holster and headed out to a meeting with the girl/woman who had left a hole in my life many years ago. She was only with me for three days, but I definitely experienced a loss. The worst was not knowing who she was, or where she went, or why she left, or whether she was dead or alive.

The address Dee Dee sent was on Rosewood Avenue, in a part of the city that had seen a more prosperous life. Now an area of low-income housing, convenience stores, little strip malls, and fast-food restaurants. I double-checked my phone because I was in front of an old used car lot that went out of business long ago. My guard went up. Anticipating a neutral location, a bar or restaurant, I drove by twice, doing some quick surveillance of the entrance and exit to the lot before turning in. I faced my BMW toward Rosewood and kept the motor running. I pulled the Beretta from my shoulder holster, clicked off the safety, and then sent Katie a text, telling her I was on site. She replied with a "thumbs-up" emoji.

Two minutes later, a black Jeep Cherokee with black rims turned in and parked near me. *Anthony DeRenzo?* The front doors opened, and two men walked over to my driver's side window. They both had their hands in the air to indicate no weapons.

"Delarosa?" one of them said.

Definitely DeRenzo doing the talking.

I lowered my window, the gun in my hand, under my jacket. "Yeah?"

"We are not armed. Here to take you to your meeting. Turn off the car."

"I can drive."

"You either come with us or the meeting is off. All there is to it. Nothing to worry about." He took a few steps back to give me distance and eliminate any threat. The other man did the same. Both still had their hands out to their sides.

"I gotta say I'm not too comfortable with this."

"Understandable, but this is the only way. She insists."

They could have killed me by now if they wanted, although Rosewood was a busy thoroughfare and it would not be my choice to kill someone in an area with security cameras on every corner and every storefront.

I turned off the engine and holstered the pistol before I climbed out.

"Got to frisk you sir. Sorry. Hands on the car."

At least he was polite, and I expected the search. He found my gun and my phone. Took my car keys, too. "Phone and keys? I need to keep in touch with my office."

"You'll get them back."

He yanked my arms back and quickly fastened a zip tie around my wrists.

I spun around. "Hey. What the hell."

"Only way, sir."

They shoved me to their vehicle and into the backseat. The second man got in the back with me and pulled a black hood over my head.

"A hood? You guys watch too much TV."

Being respectable henchmen, they kept their mouths shut. We stopped every minute or so, and I envisioned the traffic lights on Rosewood, a commercial area with plenty of cross streets. I counted four stops before turning on to what I pictured as the highway entrance. The car picked up speed, and the ride smoothed out. We continued on for a good five minutes, as best as I could calculate. I tried to count seconds, minutes, but it was hot under the hood and sweat trickled into my eyes and down the back of my neck, breaking my concentration. We slowed and came to a brief halt, and then went through three more stops and starts before the vehicle tilted downward and came to a final stop. A downtown parking garage?

The doors opened, and one man pulled me out. He took my arm and we walked, pausing for another door.

"Won't it be suspicious if someone spots you two walking a guy with a hood on his head?"

No answer.

A door hissed—an elevator. They moved me in with a bit of a shove. The door closed, a slight jerk, and the sensation of the elevator moving upward. I hoped a bell would chime as we passed each floor so I could count the floors, but it was a silent ride. We stopped; the door opened again and we only took a few steps. An electronic lock clicked, and one of the men opened another door.

They moved me forward about ten paces. We were on a hard surface, maybe hardwood. My guess—in the waiting area of an office in a high-rise?

"Don't move," DeRenzo said.

"Can you at least take off the hood?"

They didn't.

A door opened and closed.

And I waited in silent darkness. Seemed like forever but I'm sure it was less than a minute. Sweat rolled off me. I took a deep breath, making myself remain calm and focus my thoughts. I was alive, only unsure of what to expect next.

The clicking of a woman's heels on the floor was the first sound. They came closer and stopped. Was the woman in front of me? The scent of a pleasant perfume filtered through the hood. A tug at my wrists as the zip tie came off. My arms swung free, relieved to be in a normal position. A moment later, the hood gently lifted from my head.

It took a few seconds for my eyes to adjust to the light, and when I finally focused, vivid emerald eyes, cat-like eyes, now the eyes of a woman, were mere inches from mine.

"Welcome," she said.

26

It was not an office but the foyer of an exquisitely decorated apartment. She led me into a living room and offered a seat on a black leather sofa. The entire place was sleek and modern, with tables of chrome and glass, large pieces of abstract art on the walls. Draperies were closed over the windows, preventing me a peek out to get a sense of where I was in the city.

Her sleeveless, straight-line red dress stopped a few inches above her knee, accented with a black necklace and matching earrings. She poured two glasses of red wine from a bar in the corner of the room, handed me one and then sat across from me in a black leather chair, allowing the dress to ride up her bare thigh.

She caught me looking but I didn't care. There was not a man alive who would not risk a glance.

"Interesting security."

"Never can be too careful. Plus, I enjoy my privacy."

"Understandable," I said.

Her skin was as beautiful as I remembered. A perfect mix of brown and white that naturally complemented her green eyes and black hair.

"Are you as surprised as I am?"

She nodded. "Quite."

I sipped the wine. Delicious and expensive. I raised the glass. "Nice." She smiled, not saying anything. I guess waiting for me. "I looked for you for a long time. Why did you leave?"

"I was fifteen. No idea what I was doing. You saw the life I lived."

"Where did you go?"

"Well, I hitchhiked to somewhere near Philadelphia. Hung out on the street, right back to the only way I knew."

"And?" I waved my hand around. "Something happened."

"Child Services pulled me out of the gutter, literally. Weak, tired, malnourished, I had no choice but to allow them to help me. They cleaned me up, fed me, and placed me with a foster family. The people were caring, generous, and I actually went to school. For a while. Once I turned eighteen, I split, headed out on my own. Worked for an escort service, made some money. Had sworn off drugs at that point, unlike a lot of the girls, and realized I had a head for business. Got my GED, took some college classes, came back to Port City and started my own agency." She waved her hand around. "Now all this is mine."

"Every police officer has one case that stays with them forever. Usually a child who dies some needless and heartbreaking death. But you were mine. The sight of you when I first found you will never leave me. But now, I am happy. You are alive, beautiful and successful."

She laughed. "Yes, I am alive." A nostalgic tone replaced the laugh. "I did look for you."

"When?"

"After I moved back. All I remembered was your first name. I tried to find the apartment building, but I couldn't."

She pointed to a built-in bookcase behind me. I turned around. My heart jumped, and I could not believe my eyes. The pink bunny. In the center of the middle shelf. I set my wine glass on an end table, slowly stood, walked over and picked it up. The material was worn, faded, and had been sewn together in several spots. "You kept it?"

"Reminder of the one person who helped me without wanting anything in return. I always thought the foster parents considered it a job. Your motivation was genuine."

"My heart ached for you. I broke every rule, bringing you to my place. But something about you...I don't—" I stood there, holding the bunny. "I guess I can't explain it." I placed it back in its spot and sat back down. I downed the wine. "You tug at my heart like this, I'm going to need something stronger."

"What would you prefer? My bar is stocked."

"No, I'm fine."

She shifted around in the chair. Uncrossed and crossed her legs.

I couldn't take my eyes off her. She was stunning, mysterious.

"Should we talk business? You requested this meeting."

"If we must. I have a client who says he was approached by one of your employees. She threatened to expose his personal habits if he did not pay her a sum of money. Blackmail, extortion...call it what you want, but he asked for my help in resolving this dilemma."

"We can speak freely. Mr. Shelton is your client, and he hires girls through this agency."

I nodded.

"As far as Kenzie Fitzgerald—terrible what happened, but she was a troubled soul. Obviously got herself mixed up with dangerous people."

"Are you saying it was a coincidence she was dumped in front of Stan's building?"

"What else would it be? And now that she's gone, seems his problem should be over."

"He received a second call, a man demanding payment for a deal they made."

She shook her head. Shrugged. "Probably Kenzie's people."

"And he has no deal with you? Loan, investment, anything of that sort?"

"None whatsoever. And Johnny, I run a very clean business. Bills, taxes, all paid. Last thing I want is my name in the paper. Same as Mister Shelton."

I enjoyed being with her but the recent chain of events that brought me here were mind boggling, and my old friend—my instinct, my sixth sense—began to scratch at my brain.

"No doubt. And you should be proud of yourself. How you changed your life." I stood. "Thank you for seeing me. It was wonderful to learn you are alive and well."

"Leaving? I thought our reunion could continue for a while. Don't you think we owe it to each other? After all these years."

Don't do it, Delarosa. Something here does not jive. "I do, but I need to go. Another time?"

"Of course, but I am disappointed." She stood and walked me to the door.

"Is Talia your real name?"

"One of them." She flashed the brilliant smile again. With her in heels, we were eye to emerald eye. She put her arms around me, and we embraced. Then her hands were on my shoulders.

"I'm still amazed you have the bunny," I said.

"I had you with me all the time. I did not forget." She came closer, her hand on the side of my head, going through my hair. "The fifteen-year-old me had such a crush. I thought about you and cried every night, but I couldn't go back. The system frightened me. I prayed you would show up and rescue me all over again. Now that we found each other, the older me realizes just how smart the fifteen-year old was. You are a handsome man. Any family? Wife?"

"No, one ex-wife who couldn't handle being married to a cop." My hands went from her hips to the small of her back. Her eyes were mesmerizing, her perfume intoxicating.

"Her loss." She came in and pressed close, the side of her face against mine. She whispered, "You don't have to go," putting a soft kiss on my cheek.

I held her tight. "I'll regret this in a minute, but I do."

We parted.

"As you said, another time. Can I ask one favor?"

"Sure," I said.

She turned her back to me and pulled her long silky hair aside. "The zipper...could you? I always seem to have trouble."

The ultimate tease. I smiled to myself, then slowly lowered the zipper, the dress opening, revealing nothing underneath except her smooth, flawless light-brown skin. This might go down as the sexiest experience of my life.

She faced me, clutching the dress so it wouldn't fall. "You can see yourself out. The guys will take you back to your car."

I watched her walk away down a long hall, heels clicking on the hardwood, the hair partly concealing her naked back as it swished from side to side.

I reassured myself that I made the correct decision.

Someone was lying.

27

DeRenzo and his flunky picked me up as soon as I exited her apartment. The reverse of the way to Talia's: hood over my head, escorted to the car, up a ramp—which had to be a parking garage exit—through the stops and starts of downtown, out to the highway and back on Rosewood. We came to a stop on the side of the street and the man in the back with me pulled off the hood. The doors opened, we climbed out, and DeRenzo cut the zip ties and handed me back my phone, gun, and keys.

"Your car is four blocks that way." He pointed.

"Not taking me to my car?"

"End of the line for us. Have a nice night."

They got back in the Jeep and each leveled a tough-guy stare as they peeled out of the lot.

I slipped the Beretta back into my holster, then checked the phone. There were nine missed calls—and six text messages asking me to call—from Katie in the past hour. She was to notify Monica if I didn't report within two hours. The total elapsed time of my meeting with Talia, including the travel, was only ninety minutes. Something was wrong.

I called and she answered immediately. "Where are you?"

"Walking to my car." I came up to an intersection and had to find the street sign. "Uh, corner of Rosewood and Greer."

"Don't move." The call ended.

My pulse kicked up a beat as I scanned around to survey my surroundings. Standing on a corner in a lousy part of town made me feel a bit exposed.

A few seconds passed when a black Camaro stopped in front of me. The window lowered. "Get in." Monica was behind the wheel and Katie beside her. Both dressed in all black.

I hopped in the backseat. "What?"

"You are not going to be happy," Katie said.

Monica flicked on the red and blues mounted in the car's grill and we shot down Rosewood and out to the highway. Extremely uncharacteristic, especially for Katie, neither said a word.

"Where are we going and why the silence?" I asked.

"Call came on the radio an hour ago. Somebody reported an abandoned car at the old quarry," Monica said.

"And?"

"Belongs to Paul Ellison."

"Son of a bitch."

###

The old quarry, and that was how everyone referred to it ever since I could remember, located fifteen miles outside the city on Spring Hollow Road, was a working rock mine for many years, mostly producing shale. At some point, the mining company dug down too far and hit an underground stream and the giant pit filled with water, making it the place teenagers would frequent to swim, dive, and party. Fence and warning signs surrounded the property, but to teenagers, warning signs were invented to be ignored.

The place was beyond dangerous because of the jagged rocks lining the sides of the man-made crater and the unpredictable water level. But that never stopped kids from using the parking lot as a place to drink, smoke, and make out. At least once a year some kid, either drunk or high, would tempt fate and dive off the rocks and into the water forty feet below, only to never surface.

We slowed as flashing lights filled our view. Emergency vehicles and police cruisers lined the road. Monica pulled off into a grassy area on the edge of a cornfield.

"Stay here," she said. "I'll find out what I can." She got out and headed off toward a group of officers.

Katie turned to me. "Hey." She swiveled around and faced the front.

"That's it? Hey?"

"How was the meeting?" She stared out the windshield.

"Interesting. Why are you not talking?"

She turned around. "Monica. She said I talk too much and it is a sign of insecurity. So, I am making an effort to be more in control of myself, and to only talk when necessary."

"You not talking freaks me out."

"I'm trying. But I am about to explode."

"Talk before steam blows out of your ears."

"I was in your condo when Mons called, wanting you. I told her you had a meeting and she flipped out, then said she was picking me up. Here we are. She kept making me call you after I said I was to wait two hours. She is sort of intense."

"*Mons?* Yeah, she is."

"The meeting—tell me."

"DeRenzo took me to her place, not sure where, some high-rise downtown, and she denied everything. I believe she's lying and so is Shelton."

"What?"

The door opened and Monica got in. "Ellison's car is in the lot. No sign of him. They checked his apartment and now have divers in the water."

"Oh my God," Katie said. "You think he's dead?"

"We're fifteen miles outside of town. Why would he be out here? Who found the car?" I asked.

"Bunch of kids partying around a bonfire. A state trooper spotted the fire and stopped, chased off the kids, but the car stayed. He ran the tags. They came back belonging to Ellison; he called it in."

"I'll be damned. I can't imagine Ellison coming out here to what, sit and drink?"

"I agree," added Katie. "He can drink anywhere, unless he was following some lead and ended up out here questioning—"

Monica and I both held up a finger at the same time. Katie stopped.

"This will take hours. Let's go."

Monica started the Camaro and headed to Port City. I laid my head back, exhausted from a day that produced way too many surprises and evoked emotions I didn't think I had. I closed my eyes and saw nothing but the pink bunny.

28

The truth, or lack of, had kept me in business for the last six years. People lie. Lie to their spouses, employers, employees, colleagues, associates, lawyers, judges, and—believe it or not—to the police. I dealt with people who are less than forthcoming every day. Stan Shelton was holding back information, contradicting himself twice: once on whether he talked to Dee Dee on the night of Kenzie's murder, and once with the alleged blackmail scheme. Was it an extortion attempt or was he trying to wiggle out of a deal? How did I keep his name out of the news when he was not honest with me?

Talia Thorne denied any involvement with Kenzie, which I expected, and denied any business arrangements with Stan. I wanted to believe her, but my cop instinct and the voice on the phone telling Stan to stick to the arrangement were sent me a much different message.

All the thoughts on truth crowded my brain until I walked into McNally's. Mike and Katie had the local morning news on the television and the lead story was how divers found the body of Detective Paul Ellison in the old quarry last night. No details of his death and a "no comment" from PCPD, other than he dedicated his life to serving Port City for over thirty-five years, and it was a shock to everyone in the police department.

Katie saw me come in and pointed to the screen. "Can you believe this? There is no way he drove to the quarry and accidentally fell in. He was murdered. Why won't they just say it?"

"Investigation first. Evidence."

"We both know somebody did not want him working the Kenzie case." She was dressed in all black again this morning. Jeans, polo, and running shoes.

"You cannot go there without any kind of proof."

"Yeah, what if he jumped?" Mike said, jaded, but a good cop needs to ask all the questions.

Katie glared at him. "He did not commit suicide."

"Hey, maybe he thought it was a huge pool of Jack Daniels and dove in."

"You think that is funny? You're an insensitive jerk." She aimed a finger at me. "And you are not going to say anything?"

"Mike, he did not jump. Paul Ellison enjoyed the way he lived and loved a challenging case. From what I witnessed the past few days, he was full up with both."

"Yes, dear." Mike snickered. "Hold up, hold up..." Something caught his eye out our front window. "We got company."

Katie and I looked. Two black sedans on the street, definitely cops.

"Katie," I said. "Do not say a word. You are a bartender only until they leave."

"Why? I am part of this agency."

"Please." I pointed to the bar. "Go."

The expression on her face made it clear she was not happy, but she complied. The door opened and Monica Mattson walked in with Captain Elliott Lane and two other detectives behind him. The color drained from Mike's face. Either this was about Paul Ellison, or the jig was up on his friends with benefits relationship with Lane's wife. The next few minutes could define Mike's life, as in whether he lived or not.

Lane extended a hand. "McNally, how the hell are you? Haven't seen you since you retired." He was tall, well over six feet, salt-and-pepper hair, mid-fifties, lean, but a man-sized gut on him.

"Captain Elliott Lane. I'll be damned," Mike said. They shook hands.

Katie turned her back to Mike and Lane. Her jaw dropped to the floor and her eyes went huge. She mouthed, "Abby Road's husband?"

I nodded.

They talked for a minute, as if they were old pals. Mike razzing him for not coming into the bar. He eventually pointed to me.

Lane smiled and walked over and shook my hand. "Delarosa, how are you? Still getting yourself into hot water?"

"As much as I can," I said. "To what do we owe this honor?"

"I wish this was pleasure and not business, but I'm sure you heard the news about Paul Ellison?"

"Yes. Really sorry, too."

"Can we talk somewhere?"

I brought him back to my booth. Mike and Monica followed, while the other two detectives hung back, admiring the view of Katie.

"You remember Detective Mattson?"

"Sure do."

Lane's friendly attitude toward us threw me off. I thought for sure he had wind of Ellison's investigation and was about to grill me on my knowledge of Kenzie, Stan, and Entertainment Ventures.

"I took on Ellison's death myself. Want to make sure no stone is unturned."

"Smart."

"I understand he would come in here every so often."

"He did. Would stop in now and then. He was here the other day. Can't tell you how upset we are. Any leads as to what happened?"

"Not yet, but I got a real problem," he said.

"Yeah?" I thought, *here it comes*, and I sneaked a peek at Monica, who sat beside Lane in the booth. Her eyebrows arched, waiting for the hammer to fall.

"Ellison never wrote anything down. He picked up the murder of the hooker a few nights ago, but no notes, nothing. Kept it all in his head. He told some of the guys how he hung out here lately, but he left us nothing. Whatever information he had, he took it into the quarry with him. Sorry, don't mean to be crude."

Shock registered on Monica's face.

We caught such a break. That meant Lane had no clue of Stan Shelton's involvement with Fantasy Escorts or Entertainment Ventures. Or Talia.

"All we know is the dead girl worked for the escort service Monica is tracking in an investigation. If he found anything to help her, we'll never know," Lane said. "I hoped he mentioned something to you guys."

"I wish, but he never talked shop. All social, except about him retiring. Sad. What's your gut telling you?" Mike asked.

Lane shook his head. "Got drunk and wandered off the edge. Why he was there is a mystery. Anything comes your way, give me a call?" He threw down a business card.

"Sure, sure." Mike squeezed out of the booth and we followed. "Captain, huh?"

"Wonders never cease." He slapped Mike on the shoulder and then handshakes all around.

I patted a barstool. "Got a seat for you, anytime."

"Be careful, might take you up on that." Lane and the other detectives went out.

Mike went back to the booth and collapsed on the bench with his head on the table. "Oh my God."

"You are one lucky son-of-a-bitch." I slid Lane's business card to him. "You want this souvenir? Stick it on the refrigerator?"

Katie came over, her hands on her hips. "Sweating, weren't you?"

Monica said, "Am I missing something?"

29

"To Ellison," we all shouted as we each threw back a shot of Jack Daniels in his honor. Mike, Katie, Monica, and I stood around the bar and thought it was the least we could do for taking my client off the hook and the front page. More importantly, he was a damn good cop.

"Shelton is charmed," Mike proclaimed, as he helped himself to a second shot. "My God, first the girl who was supposedly blackmailing him is murdered, end of the blackmail, and now the detective putting this puzzle together is also dead. Either Stan is killing them himself, or he is charmed."

"And he is nothing but walking contradictions. The story changes with each conversation. If I didn't listen to the last call myself, I would dump him," I said.

"What about the woman who owns the escort service?" he asked.

"She denies any involvement with Stan, other than him being a client, or Kenzie. She passed her off as a troubled soul, mixed up with the wrong people. But there is something with this woman, Talia. Too guarded, secretive. I had one of my feelings."

"Well, those feelings served you well over the years. Tell me how I can help. Right now, though, I got to open this joint." Mike offered another round and we all partook. He unlocked the front door, as Katie, Monica and I retreated to my booth. Katie opened her laptop for a check on Stan's car.

"What I'm lacking is insight into the escort business. How it works, how these girls are hired."

Katie snickered. "Mons, you have come to the right place."

"Follow me," I said.

We scooted out of the booth and headed for the back door when Katie stopped us. "Wait, wait. He's on the move, south of the city." She moved the computer around for us to observe.

"We'll call him from the car. So much for him staying home."

We rode in my BMW, and I connected the phone to the car's speaker system.

He answered on the first ring. "Johnny, boy, how the hell are you?"

"I'm fine, Stan. I hoped we could meet later."

"Can't today. I'm on my way to a golf outing in Myrtle Beach. Benefit for old NFL players and their health and welfare fund."

"Myrtle Beach? When are you coming back?"

"Tonight. Quick trip."

"Are you at the airport?"

"Hell no, on my way to Davis Airfield. I keep my plane there. We'll shoot down, I'll do my thing, and come up tonight. Only way to go."

"You own a plane?"

"Beechcraft six-seater. Gorgeous."

"Remember I wanted you to stay home?"

"Can't cancel this one. I booked it months ago. Sorry, but we'll be back tonight."

"We'll talk tomorrow." I closed the call. "So much for him staying home. I had no idea he had a plane."

"I don't envy you. He'll be tough to wrangle in," she said. "Wrangle in the truth, too."

Club Cuba enjoyed a reputation as one of Port City's premiere restaurants and supper clubs. Great food from a James Beard award-winning chef and the hottest Latin bands in the area, made reservations a two-month wait, all because of the class and dedication and the owner, Leah Love. I told Monica the story of Leah and our relationship, and how I fell in love with her on the night I arrested her for running an illegal, high-class, call-girl ring. These were the days before escort services legitimized, or masked, the real business. When the heat was turned high on her business, she walked away with a lot of cash and set her sights on nightclubs.

Leah and I had an understanding. More like a long-distance relationship, even though we lived in the same city. She enjoyed her life as an entrepreneur, fulfilled by the work and her customers, and I enjoyed my independence. About once a month, we met for an evening of dinner, drinks, dancing, and a night cap at her place in the exclusive, oceanfront Atlantic Shores building. We would update each other on our lives and talk about the future we both wanted, but not now.

"Sounds like the perfect arrangement to me," Monica said.

"It works for us."

We pulled into the lot and parked. The restaurant did not open until four, but Leah was always in early to handle the admin tasks.

Julio, her bar manager, waved as we walked through headed to her office. The door was opened but I announced us with a knock. She was in jeans and a white blouse, her black hair pulled back. But no matter what she wore, she was still the most beautiful woman I ever encountered. She removed her reading glasses and greeted me with a hug.

"Leah, meet Detective Monica Mattson."

They shook hands, and we all took seats around a small coffee table. Leah was always the warmest, engaging, and most welcoming person in the room. It was what made her club so successful. She introduced herself to each guest and told them she would take care of their every need personally if she had to. It kept them coming back, time after time.

But I immediately sensed her guard went up when meeting Monica. Was it a natural reaction when two beautiful, successful, and confident women were put together in a room? Or was this Leah's natural response to being in the presence of a cop? She told me hundreds of times she had an inherent distrust of police, and that I was her exception to the rule. She said she tuned in to my tendency to bend the rules, much like the way Talia Thorne loved how I "stuck it to the man" by shielding her from Child Services.

They locked eyes and I sensed it was two females sizing each other up. It was in my best interest to break the staring contest and get the party started. "Leah, Monica is working a sex trafficking case where girls are moved through Port City on their way to New York. A local escort service, Fantasy Escorts, popped on her radar as possible facilitators. In your past life, ever run into any traffickers? We were hoping you could shed some light on the escort business and how they could be involved."

"Are you working this, too?" she asked, pointedly, staring at me.

"No. I have a client who got himself in hot water hiring girls from Fantasy. Our paths crossed during the investigation."

Monica nodded. "I hadn't seen John in years." She put a hand on my shoulder and held it there for a moment. "We were both so surprised to see each other again. He was the only detective I respected, and trusted. For many years, I always wanted to work with him. And now's my chance."

Oh boy. None of what she said, and did, was necessary. I wondered whether she fired a shot across the bow, only to provoke a reaction.

Leah's response was diplomatic but loaded. "Good for you. He is a thorough detective. My experience with...John...has been more than satisfying. Now, how can I help you?"

"Recruiting girls. Was it difficult?"

"No. I only advertised once, when I began the agency. After that, it was all word of mouth."

"You screen these girls prior to hiring them?"

"Yes, and you'd be surprised. Most came from nice homes and backgrounds. No street trash worked for me."

"You had a reputation," Monica added.

"Damn right."

"Ever approached by traffickers?"

"Yes. By some Haitians. Once. Wanted me to keep girls for a while before they were sent to other cities. Much the same as what you are working on. Acclimate them to a new life in the States, and then send them to the bright lights of New York."

"And?"

"I threw them out of my office. Unfortunately, one of my guys had to reinforce the message."

"She has a team of security pros who lend a hand when needed," I added.

"I see," Monica said. "Any idea how the girls were to be transported?"

"Not, really. My understanding, and this is only from what I read, girls—and boys too, don't forget—come across the border in Texas, and then are brought up the East Coast. In the case of the Haitians, they fly them into Florida and drive up."

"We figured as much. Just trying to get a handle. These folks always seem to be one step ahead."

"Sure are," she said. "A lot of money involved, money the girls never see."

"Copy that," Monica said, forgetting she was the only cop in the room. "So, you never hired girls who came through traffickers, to your knowledge?"

Leah paused and slowly shook her head. My guess was she was counting to ten. "Never. I wish I could be of more help."

"Me too. Nice to meet you. Cool place you have here. I need to come back."

"I'll have a table waiting."

We all stood. They shook hands and Leah and I hugged. Monica and I started for the door, but Leah stopped us. "Johnny, got a second?" Monica took the hint and kept going.

"Sure."

Leah grabbed me around my neck and kissed me full on the mouth like I've never been kissed before. "That's a reminder."

"I don't need a reminder," I said.

"She might."

I stared into the gorgeous dark eyes and thought the less said the better.

30

"What was the bit with your hand on my shoulder? If you wanted to send a message, it worked." Monica and I were in my car, headed back to McNally's.

"What are you talking about?"

"You were flirty."

"She's grown. I'm only helping your relationship. Going on a date once a month might work for you two, but it leaves twenty-nine other days in the month for someone else to pay attention. And her, too. If I stir the pot, one of you will realize you need to increase the dates to two or three a month."

"Or, you enjoy keeping everyone off-balance. Leave some friction in your wake."

"Or, I can take one of those twenty-nine days. You don't think men hit on her? What does she do with her non-Johnny days?"

"We are fine and secure in our relationship, and I don't need you to create a problem where there isn't one."

"I apologize. But if I want something, I don't hesitate."

People do not change, including her. This was always the issue with Mad Dog, and it made her unlikable with many officers. She had her own set of rules and achieved results, but many times at a high cost. She would march into a situation, create havoc, obtain what she wanted, and leave as if nothing happened.

Saying nothing at this point was best, but I was not going to stew in curiosity. "What do you want?"

"Huh?"

"What is it you want?"

She smiled. "You want to talk about this now?"

"You started it."

"Hey, no secret I always had a thing for you. I think you felt the same. We never got there, for whatever reason. Working together again brought it all back and meeting Leah motivated me. No ring on her finger, Delarosa."

Was this her creating havoc only to leave later or was she serious? I glanced at her. The window was half-open, allowing the wind to toss her black hair around her sexy, freckled face. *Damn.* She was such an enigma for so many of us, and now do I have a chance to crack the code? *Keep your head, Delarosa.*

We drove in silence for a few miles until her cell rang.

"Sure, Gil. I can meet in thirty minutes." She held the phone down from her face, and asked me, "The FBI. Mind if we meet at McNally's?"

"Sure, fine."

She gave the agent the address and ended the call. "Thanks. He has new information on the sex trafficking. I want you to sit in on the meeting."

"He'll never allow me in. Plus, I should duck out at this point. It is your case, not sure how I can help."

"Johnny, if this is about the conversation we just had, please pull over so I can shoot you right here."

"No, it is not." We stopped at a light. "My client is nothing but contradictions. We can press him, but I don't want to tip off Talia, and we don't know if there is anything there or not."

"But it's all we have."

I lowered my sunglasses and looked her dead in the eye. "Besides, I'm too much man for you anyhow."

"Oh, Delarosa." She hit me in the arm. "Game on, stud."

A horn blared behind us. The light had turned green. "Shall we go, Mad Dog?"

"You have yet to experience how mad this dog can be."

###

FBI Special Agent Gil Evans stood five foot seven on a good day. Slight of build, thinning brown hair, his weapon had to weigh more than he did. He was all business, though—got straight to the point with his intelligence.

We gathered in my booth, and much to his reluctance, I had Katie take notes. Monica convinced him I had information that could open a door for us into Entertainment Ventures.

"The Texas Border Patrol reports at least a dozen girls were smuggled into the Houston area last week," he explained. "They crossed over somewhere near Laredo, safe harbored in either San Antonio or Corpus Christi for a few days, then moved to Houston. From there, we were able to track four girls into Atlanta, then lost them. We want to stop them in Port City, squeeze the bottleneck south—Atlanta, then Texas, so forth."

"All teenagers?" Monica asked. "And all will be forced into prostitution?"

"Mostly teens, some in their twenties. Not always into prostitution. Many into forced labor or domestic servitude. Yes, in this country. Not just cities, either. Some are fanned out to small towns and rural areas to work basically as slaves on farms or in homes as maids, domestics, or nannies. Travel documents are confiscated so they can't leave."

"Unbelievable. How can we help?" I asked.

"Detective Mattson tells me you might have a lead into Fantasy Escorts?"

"Yes. Flimsy, though," I said.

"Mr. Delarosa agreed to do what he can. Best angle we have so far," Monica said.

"The focus is on their travel from Atlanta north, which should happen in the next few days. Anything you can add will be helpful at this point. Information only." He focused on Monica. "Please do not take any actions." Then back to me. "Your involvement is off the record?"

"For now. My priority is to help my client. I'll turn over what I can without exposing him. If he is complicit, I am happy to turn him over."

"Fair enough. The bureau thanks you. You can reach me through Detective Mattson."

Agent Evans departed.

"I can't believe Mister Shelton would be involved in human trafficking. Even though he is a pig, in my opinion," Katie added, as she closed her laptop.

"Did something happen?" Monica asked.

"Hell yes. We had a group of guys in here and in comes the football hero—"

I stopped her. "Not the time."

"Girl talk, later," Monica said, winked at her.

"Yes, but I still think he's too dumb to be involved in trafficking." She got out of the booth. "Mike needs me." She pointed a finger at both of us. "I want more street time. I need my hours if I'm ever to get my license. Don't leave me sitting here."

"Yes, bad ass," Monica said.

"I mean it." She went into the kitchen.

"Entertaining, isn't she?"

I nodded. "Oh yeah. What's the plan, Detective?"

"I hoped you had one. Call you later." She slid out.

"Where are you going?"

"I promise Robbery I'd help run warrants. Shouldn't be too long." She went out through the rear door.

I sat in thought for a while. Was Katie correct? Was Stan too dumb to be involved in human trafficking, or did he allow himself to be seduced deep into a criminal enterprise that had no exit? If he did not come clean with me and allow my help, even the Shelton way—the glad-handing over-the-top bullshit—wouldn't save him.

31

The lunch traffic in McNally's tapered off, so I decided a mental health break was in order, at least my version, which consists of a handsome bottle of Woodford Reserve bourbon and a Dave Koz CD in the player. I poured a hearty shot into a glass and sat back on the sofa with my feet propped on the coffee table. Monica's flirty jab during our meeting bothered me. The last thing I needed was Leah friction. Was it a genuine attraction that resurfaced for Monica, or her twisted way of endearing herself to me to gain an advantage on what could lead to her breaking the case? I had to remind myself, a second time, her caustic nature was her style—use any means necessary to sharpen an angle.

The GPS on Stan's car reported he traveled from Davis Airfield at ten o'clock the previous night and went straight home. Down and back in one day, as he said. He was on my agenda for the day, along with his paramour, Dee Dee. I thought I would fire a shot across her bow to provoke a response. The two meetings with her were as if I met with two different women. First, she was scared and wanted protection, to the second meeting where her flirting was as blatant and obvious as her motive. It did not take a seasoned private eye to figure out she only wanted to compromise my investigation. Why, though?

Drink number two went down as smooth as the first. I stretched out on the sofa as Dave Koz's saxophone launched into, "Life in the Fast Lane," the soundtrack for the Stan Shelton lifestyle: traveling in the fast lane with no exit ramp in sight.

I sent him a text, asking to meet.

I searched Myrtle Beach golf courses on my phone and called one at random.

"Pro shop," a girl answered.

"Hi, is this the course where the NFL players are having a tournament?" I asked.

"Umm, hold on." She came back a few seconds later. "That was yesterday at Shoreline Golf Club."

"Oh gosh, I'm a day late. Thanks."

Never hurt to follow up on a client. Stan had too many question marks swirling around his head for me to neglect my due diligence.

The next shot was at Dee Dee. No texting—I called; she answered after two rings.

"This is a surprise," she said. "New information on the case?"

"Sorry, nothing new. I was wondering if we could continue the conversation from the other night?"

"Well, aren't you the mystery man. I would love to."

"Not sure about any mystery. Free tonight? Meet you at Joey Mac's?"

"Perfect. Eight o'clock?"

"See you then."

Third on the agenda was the toughest. Talia Thorne. No phone number. I never asked and I doubt she would share it anyhow. Hell, she had her goons bring me to her place quite literally under the cloak of darkness. I would find my way into her world. She could try to operate in the dark if she wanted, but what was done in the dark always found the light.

Koz was in the groove. I stretched out on my sofa just as his, "Lullaby for A Rainy Night" filled the room, and prayed for the soul of Paul Ellison.

"Johnny, hey." Katie's voice.

My eyes opened; blonde hair hovered above me. She shook my shoulder and it took a moment to focus. "Katie?"

"Damn, you were out. Slept through my calls."

"What time is it?"

"Two." She checked my phone. "You missed a call from Monica, who is on her way, and one from Shelton."

"I'll call him back as soon as I can think."

"No need. He's downstairs, holding two guys hostage with some ridiculous story about him, a running back, and three pro cheerleaders."

"Are you kidding? Can you bring him up?"

"If I can pull him away."

"Throw an extra swivel in your hips, he'll follow you anywhere."

"Shut up."

I headed for the bathroom to splash water on my face to wake up from the bourbon-induced coma.

"Drink, Stan?"

Katie had successfully lured the raconteur from his audience.

"Why not." I poured two, handed him one. "I got your text and thought, hell, instead of responding, I will just pop in, see what is new with my favorite PI."

"Glad you did. How was the tournament yesterday?"

"Wonderful. Great to hang with some of the old guys. Golf game sucked. Can't drink and play at the same time. So, I drink and pretend at golf. I used to drink and play football. Played my best games hammered. Did I ever tell you about the time we were in Kansas City—"

"Whoa, Stan, hold up. I'd love to listen, but once you get rolling, it's hard to bring the big train to a stop."

He laughed. "Another time. But after all this mess is over, you and I hit the town. My treat."

"You're on. Tell me about your plane though. You own it?"

"Smartest money I ever spent. We use it for all our travel on the East Coast. Yesterday, less than two hours down, then came right back last night."

"Nikki go too?"

"Hell yeah, she loves those events—all the pretty people, media. She eats it up. Plus, the real reason, I tend to get attention from the ladies, and if she's around, they back off. Prevents a lot of strife."

"What problems you have." My phone buzzed, a text from Monica.

"Can I come up?"

"No, we'll be down, and you are NOT a cop around him."

"Copy."

"Ready?" I said. His behavior was bizarre to me. *Did he forget about the second phone call?*

"For what?"

"The phone call? You were to transfer money today." *Does his mind block out the things he wants to avoid, and only allow him to concentrate on the past, where he can glorify his exploits? Or did he take one too many shots to the head?*

"Shit, Johnny. Everything I got going on...did you talk to them? Did you?" His face reddened, eyes went to the floor. "I can't transfer any money. It will expose me. I'll be shit. Nikki will divorce me if she ever finds out what I did. Can you call? Buy us some time."

I opened my notepad to the number and used one of my burners and called. A messaged played: "This phone number is no longer in service."

"Now what do we do?" he asked, his eyes huge, pleading.

"What you do best. We go on offense."

32

A cheer went up from four guys at a table when Stan and I walked into McNally's. Monica had a spot at the bar, chatting with Mike. I introduced her as my friend.

"Any friend of Johnny's is a friend of mine. What are you drinking, sweetheart? I'm buying."

"Thanks, nothing for me. Only stopped in to say hello to John."

The group of guys called for Stan.

"My public awaits. You are welcome to join us."

She smiled. "Something tells me I am much safer here on my stool."

He put a hand on my shoulder. "Offer stands, but I got to say, my man here keeps himself surrounded by beautiful women. Between you and her"—he pointed to Katie—"damn, John, you have excellent taste. I love my blondie over there, but the freckles on this filly are some of the sexiest I ever laid eyes on."

Katie ignored him. I figured Monica would shoot him on the spot, but she surprised me.

"Why, thank you, Mister Shelton. Maybe I should join you. I love a man who appreciates an attractive woman."

He shouted to the guys, "Boys, hold tight while the master goes to work."

Mike and Katie stopped what they were doing. She picked up the TV remote and muted the sound. The men went silent. I glanced at Mike and his eyebrows were popped.

Oh God.

Monica remained on the stool. She grabbed the collar of his sport coat, pulled him down to her and whispered into his ear.

His eyes went wide, his face got red, and his head bobbed up and down. He didn't say one word.

After a minute or so, she let go of his jacket and he straightened. And for the first time in forever, he was silent. Rivulets of sweat ran down the side of his face. He pointed to the back of the bar.

"Leaving, Stan?"

He nodded.

I walked a few steps with him. "Go home and stay there. I need to think about our next move. If they call again, message me immediately. Do not leave your house."

All he did was nod. He grabbed my hand with both of his and shook it, then went out. The room was quiet. T he four guys asked for their check. Katie beamed from ear to ear.

"Mad Dog," I said. "We'll never know, will we?"

"Nope."

"Want to go for a ride?"

"Sure."

Davis Airfield was twenty-five miles south of town and not too far from my cottage on Crescent Beach.

"Why are we here again?" Monica asked.

"Hunch."

"A smart detective never ignores a hunch."

"Take off your blazer and holster. We are a couple inquiring about flying lessons. Don't need anyone to smell a cop."

"Copy that, ten-four, roger."

"Wise ass."

We parked in front of a small, one-story, white cinder block building, and went inside to an open space that had a counter, sitting area with sofas surrounding a table, a TV monitor on the wall displaying the local weather radar, four vending machines, and a trolley with a coffeemaker. Behind the counter were floor-to-ceiling windows. Brochures advertised flying lessons. *First Lesson Free!* No employees inside, so we ventured out through a side door that opened to the tarmac.

Single-engine planes lined the length of a blacktop runway. My aircraft knowledge was limited, but I guessed Cessnas and Pipers. Portable canopies covered a few and I noticed they were all anchored in place. To the left of the main building were the two hanger-like structures. On the first was a sign: Shelton Flight Services.

"The sign," I said. "Shelton."

"Duly noted. That the hunch?"

"Could be. You ever fly in one of these small things?"

"A couple times," she said. "Kind of fun. You?"

"No, I got a thing about heights. I need to be in a jet with flight attendants who serve drinks."

"Sissy."

A man came out of the building and spotted us, waved, and he walked up. "Hi there, Bill Davis. How can I help you?" He was about six one, my height, but had a rotund belly, full head of white hair with a matching long beard. Easily a mall Santa at Christmas.

"I'm, John...my wife Monica. Curious about flying lessons. We haven't the first clue. Always been a bucket list thing for her."

"You are in the right place, come on in."

We went inside and he began the lesson spiel. Ground school classroom instructions, training hours needed, the expense, medical requirements, all leading up to the first solo flight.

"What do you think, honey?"

"This is all exciting. I'm not sure. Are you the instructor?" she said to Bill.

"Not anymore. Cataracts in one eye got me grounded. We have two other young guys who teach. Excellent pilots, years of experience—both learned to fly in the military. Bobby and Tony."

"You own all this? You said your name is Davis?"

"Used to. I still have all the land, just sold the flight operations business."

"I saw the sign. Shelton Flight Operations? Is that Stan Shelton?"

"Yep. The football player, owns the car dealerships."

"Of course. He flies, too?"

"No, he keeps Bobby on call, mostly. Busy guy, always going somewhere. Fun, though. He comes out here, hangs around, telling stories. Checks on the business. When that good old boy gets wound up talking, hoo wee. He can't stop."

"I met him at a party once. He is a character."

"Oh yeah. That's his plane over there. The twin-engine Beechcraft." He pointed through the window.

"It's bigger than the others. How many seats?" Monica asked.

"Six. Real beauty. He gets his money's worth, too."

"Very cool. Honey, you get your license, and we'll buy one of those and you can be my private pilot," I said.

"Wouldn't you love that." She jabbed my ribs with an elbow.

"Hey, we have plenty of women come here and learn."

"See," I said. "Bill, what is the flight-based operations?"

"Sells all the fuel and maintenance. The mechanics work for him. And the flying lessons are his, too. Plus, he plans to build three hangers, so he'll be able to rent space to pilots. Guys around here love him because a decent injection of cash has been needed for a long time. Can be lucrative if we stay busy."

"Interesting. Well, a lot for us to digest, right, sweetie?"

"Quite a bit. Who are the instructors again?"

"Bobby Rodriguez and Tony DeRenzo." He handed us business cards and we thanked him.

As we got in the car, I scanned around for the black Jeep Cherokee. Nothing. "I love it when a hunch pays off, and this one paid way more than I expected."

"DeRenzo?"

"Yes. Are you thinking what I am thinking? We need to talk to a pilot. I have a thousand questions."

"I am calling a friend of mine who flies. And by the way, luckily for you the hunch paid off, because if you called me honey or sweetie one more time, you were going to get your wings clipped."

33

The meeting of the brain trust convened promptly at six o'clock in the ultra-secure isolation of the back booth of McNally's Irish Pub. In attendance were Detective Monica Mattson of the PCPD, apprentice private investigator Katie Pitts, and me. Carlos Suarez, our part-time bartender and cook was handling the bar duties, so Katie was free to and dig in and earn the hours needed to obtain her PI license. As soon as I told her I wanted her in the meeting with Monica and me, she changed from her jeans and T-shirt into her all-black outfit.

"Any update with your pilot friend?"

"Tomorrow at ten," Monica said. We had already briefed Katie on our excursion to the airfield and discovering Anthony DeRenzo is a pilot.

"So, they could be flying girls to Port City from Atlanta?" Katie asked, as she typed away on the laptop.

"Possible. Seems it would be easy to track, though. My understanding is all flights need to register a flight plan."

Katie stopped typing. "I read once where the Mexican drug cartels fly drugs across the Caribbean Sea and the pilots stay under the radar."

Was flying under the radar actually possible? "You read this where?" I asked.

"No idea. Sometime in college."

"Monica, a question for your pilot friend."

"Katie is correct. They can fly low. Not sure about flying up the East Coast with the Coast Guard monitoring air traffic. We'll find out. Let's switch to land. What did you find on the trucking companies?"

Katie opened a file on the laptop. "A lot of information on the two you gave me, but nothing that would raise any flags as far as I could tell. Hit the Road Trucking carries consumer goods to the North and Northeast, using regular eighteen wheelers. Deep South Trucking hauls steel from Birmingham to the Northeast and lumber all over the country. They use flatbeds. I don't know how to search for anything suspicious."

"Do they both drive routes through Port City?" asked Monica.

"Not sure. I found out trucks are equipped with ELDs—electronic logging devices that track the truck's movements and hours driven. We would need access to the logs. And you asked for names of drivers, and none of that is online. I say we hack in, access their drivers' contracts and run background checks."

"We need warrants to legally hack, and we don't have probable cause. I don't know any hackers with those skills," Monica added.

Katie and I exchanged a glance. We worked with a kid not long ago who could hack into any site anywhere. He paid a price and swore off hacking. Plus, he was somewhere in California touring with his band.

"Forget it, it is a long-shot lead from the FBI. Something tipped them to those two companies, so let them follow up. Our best bet is to stay focused here," Monica said. "I'm intrigued by the flying aspect. Nothing new—traffickers use any means necessary, but now we add names to the equation."

"Wait...yeah, this is perfect. Mons, close your ears. What are the chances we can stick a tracker on Anthony's car?" Katie asked. "We then follow him, and when he is at the airfield, put some eyeballs on the action."

"Eyeballs on the action?" I asked.

"Sure, surveillance. Duh."

Mad Dog giggled at her. "Yeah, Johnny, surveillance."

"Katie, you have the solution for Anthony's car," I said.

"I do?"

I nodded. "Details when our detective friend can't hear us. The less she knows, the better. On to the meeting tonight with Dee Dee. How hard do I press? In my two meetings with her, I bet she has yet to tell the truth."

"Hard. Tell her the cops are all over the trafficking and she needs to come clean or you will serve her up."

"I'm not sure. She links Stan to the business and is also the connection to Anthony and Talia. If we spook her now, it might kill any angle into their organization," I said.

"Fair point. Make Stan the weak link. Tell her you are worried about his mental state and that he is threatening to do something stupid," Monica said. "The phone call said he needed to complete the deal. If he won't fess up to it, maybe she will."

"Depends which Dee Dee shows up." My phone rang, Stan's name on the screen. "Stan?" I pressed the speaker for Monica and Katie to listen.

"They just called again, Johnny." His voice was animated. "They want the transfer today or something bad will happen. No more of putting my name in the papers— said this has now escalated and I will pay a steep price if I don't follow through."

"Where are you?" I motioned to Katie to pull up his GPS.

"Home. What do we do?"

"Stay put. Give me some time."

Katie showed me her computer screen. His car was at his house. "I will call you later. And don't worry." I ended the call. "Just because the car is there doesn't mean he is."

"He sounded scared," Katie said. "Do you think they're serious?"

"Might be a bluff," Monica added. "If he is the money, they need him."

"Yeah, why cut off the source?" I sat for a second. Both stared at me, waiting for me to talk. "Bad Ass One and Bad Ass Two. I hope you are ready, because we have work to do."

34

"You surprised me," Dee Dee said, as she sat down at the table in Joey Mac's. Across from me this time, not beside me as she did in our second meeting.

"Why?"

"I said our paths would cross again but I didn't think so soon. I thought I blew it the other night. My intentions were obvious, but you didn't bite."

"We have another matter to clear up first. Plenty of time for me to bite later."

She laughed. "Fair enough, but I hope nothing too serious."

"Our friend, Stan. Who is extorting him?"

"Whoa, right down to business. Didn't even order a drink yet."

I waved to Joey, and he stopped at our table.

"Vodka, with some ice," she said. He went off. "Extorting? I thought all that died with Kenzie."

"He received another call, asking him to complete the deal. What deal did he make and with whom? I think you know."

She shook her head. "No idea."

"He never told you? Confided? Confessed his secrets?"

"No. He is your client—ask him."

"I have, but he denies any deal." I paused, leaned across the table a bit and lowered my voice, hoping to pull her into my confidence. "He is embarrassed, and I'm worried about him. The stress is causing erratic behavior and I'm afraid he might do something stupid."

"Stupid how?"

"Panic. Go to the police. I tell him to stay home and then I find out he is flying down South to some golf tournament. I didn't even know he owned a plane."

She paused. *To register the fact that I was now aware of the plane?* "Yeah, he is unpredictable. We'll have a date set up, and he won't show. It happened a few times."

"Help me protect him from himself. Can you remember anything Kenzie might have said?"

"No, I swear. She was scared, but it was her own doing. She obviously cooked up a plan with some nasty people. I am sorry. Not sure what else I can say."

"He is the one who is scared. He tells me there is no deal, only the demand for him to pay, or be exposed to the world. He is not a bad guy, just a reckless juvenile. A big kid with money. I want to help him, but to do that, I need you to tell me everything you can about Kenzie. Friends, clients, anything. I need a name."

I sensed her frustration. She sipped her vodka and sat back with her arms folded. Defensive body language and for all the playacting she did on a nightly basis, this performance was not creative at all. She could do better. And she tried.

"The first time you and I met, I was frightened. Kenzie was dead, and I remembered how she told me to stay out of her business. Then, after the meeting with you, I realized her life had nothing to do with mine. Sure, we compared our regulars all the time, including Stan. No secret he's loaded, so maybe her harebrained idea sprang from there. She likely seduced some scumbag into making the phone calls, told him there would be a payday. Other than that, I don't know any of her friends."

"Who would be calling him now?"

"Same said scumbag."

"Trying to work the scam himself? He told Stan to transfer money to a bank that is registered in the Cayman Islands. A bit more complicated than handing over cash to some punk on the corner. I listened to the second call and it sounded as if he agreed to a deal. What about Talia? Could he have made a deal with her?"

"Talia? I'm not privileged to company business."

"You two never talk shop?"

She stiffened in her seat; her eyes hardened. "Gee, we are a long way from me flirting and hoping to go back to your place. Did you meet with her?"

"Yes, and I want another meeting. And I want you to set it up."

"No, none of this concerns me."

My frustration was now on the rise. "Talia, Stan, Kenzie, her accomplice—all are spokes on a wheel. And guess where you are? The hub. The bull's-eye. Smack in the middle. Everything connects to you. If he did agree to some money deal, that's on him. But the extortion ends now. Or, I bring in the cops on the blackmail of a Fantasy Escorts client, and your name will be front and center. Daniella "Dee Dee" DeRenzo. Sorry, it's a dirty world, and the cops love a juicy hooker-celebrity case. Ask Paul Ellison. Oh, wait, he's dead, and I guarantee it was not a suicide. Get in front of this now."

"A threat? Not very becoming."

"Not out to hurt you. A name, and time with Talia, and I keep you out of it."

The flirty woman from two nights ago was gone. She was expressionless, her eyes examining mine. Calculating what to show and what to hold. "She used to buy drugs from a guy. Lamar Shanks." She finished off the vodka in one gulp and stood. "You didn't hear it from me."

"Understood. The meeting?"

She pulled a twenty from her purse, threw it on the table and walked out.

I sent a text to Katie. "She's leaving."

Joey came over and put a hand on my shoulder. "I don't think you two are friends anymore."

"A blessing, paisan, a blessing."

Monica and Katie picked me up in the alley behind Joey Mac's. "Well?"

"A car service both ways," Katie said.

"I figured as much. Ready for job number two?"

###

We were in Monica's Camaro with her driving, me shotgun, and Katie and her long legs scrunched up in the back. We parked a half-block away from Mrs. DeRenzo's rowhouse. The call needed to be made in proximity to the house in case it would be traced.

Katie called 9-1-1. "Yes, I am in front of 1148 Twenty-Seventh Street, and there is smoke coming out of the roof. No, I can't see any flames, but a lot of smoke. I can hardly breathe. My name? Bernadette Wojokowski. Okay, thanks." She closed the burner flip phone.

"Bernadette Wojokowski? What?" Monica asked. "How did you come up with that name?"

"We were best friends, but her family moved to Chicago the summer after sixth grade. We decided to be pen pals and wrote letters each week—"

"Katie. Later," I snapped. "Careful with the names. Never use anything that can be linked back to you."

"Okay, geez."

Within four minutes, three fire engines roared down Twenty-Seventh and converged in front of the DeRenzo residence. Firemen hopped off the trucks and went to work, pulling hoses. Two pounded on her door. An upstairs light blinked on and seconds later, she opened the door. Spotlights turned night into day as curious neighbors poured from their homes, many in robes covering their nightclothes. A ladder reached from a truck to the roof of her house.

Two firefighters escorted Mrs. DeRenzo, in her housecoat, away from the action. She had a phone up to her ear while she watched men carefully traverse the ladder to her roof.

Firemen climbed around on the roof, searching for a source to the nonexistent fire. Eight minutes had elapsed when a black Jeep Cherokee with black rims screeched to a halt in the middle of the street. Anthony DeRenzo jumped out and ran to his mother.

"Go, now," I said. Katie pulled her black ski cap over her head, tucking her blonde hair underneath. "Now. You should already have the cap on."

I opened the car door, and she squeezed out from the back, trotted to the left rear fender of the Jeep, ducked down, and placed the GPS tracker, secured in a magnetized housing, in the wheel well.

"Unbelievable. You know how many laws you two broke?" Monica asked.

"At least three."

"Try four. And I love it."

Katie was back in the car in less than thirty seconds. "Okay?"

"Perfect," I said. "You are becoming quite proficient."

"At breaking the law," Detective Mattson scolded.

Anthony DeRenzo's arms flailed in the middle of a circle of firefighters as neighbors crowded around. I'm sure he demanded answers, as in someone needs to pay for this prank.

"Monica?" I said.

"Yes?"

"You can drive now."

35

DEA Agent Nick Villano walked into McNally's at exactly 10:00 a.m. as scheduled. I unlocked the door a few minutes earlier when Monica arrived. Over six feet tall, broad shouldered, muscular, and a flat stomach. I hated him already. He sported an old-fashioned flat-top haircut and had his sunglasses parked on top of his head. In a T-shirt, jeans, and tattoos covering both arms, he was a walking recruiting poster for the military—my guess, a Marine. He gripped my hand with a bone-breaking handshake, and I thought I would never want to be on his bad side.

"Nice to meet you, sir. How can I help?" he said.

Monica filled him in on the sex trafficking case and how our investigations crossed. Also, my background as a detective before going private. Then provided a bit of his resume in the Navy—my guess was wrong—as a pilot.

"Can a plane fly at a low altitude, undetected by radar, is our question. We believe the girls—and it's all speculation at this point—are being flown to Davis Airfield by a six-seat Beechcraft," I asked.

"Sure, happens all the time. On the East Coast of the US, planes are not really undetected by radar, but if they turn off the transponder and maintain a low altitude, it can be done. It would take an experienced pilot familiar with the terrain. People moving drugs, or in your case, people, can be very creative."

"Transponder?"

"All planes have one. It sends and receives signals to air traffic control. That's how the controllers identify the plane and its location."

"And if it is turned off?"

"You are on your own. Stay less than three thousand feet, don't run into the mountains coming up the eastern part of the county. The problem is, with the transponder off, they can't find you if you get in trouble."

When she first mentioned him, I wondered whether he and Monica had a past, but he came off as an ultra-square, follow the rules type, which would not mesh with her roughshod, break all the rules style.

"Davis, huh?" he said. "Bill Davis trained me for my private pilot's license when I was seventeen. Excellent pilot, one of my favorite people. I stop out every so often to say hello. He could answer all these questions."

"We met him, but only to check out the place. We were a couple interested in flying lessons," Monica said. "He has a pilot there we suspect."

"Copy that. Damn, Bill is an upstanding guy. If he found out his airstrip was used for trafficking, he'd shoot those guys himself and then call the cops."

"Want a coffee? We have stronger."

"No thank you, sir. I need to be going anyhow." We all slid out of the booth. "Monica, Beth says hello."

"Give her my best," she said.

They hugged, then he squeezed the life out of my right hand, flipped down his sunglasses, and was out the door.

"Is Beth his wife?" I asked.

"Yeah, why?"

"No reason...just wondering. Seems like a nice guy." I sat down.

She put her palms on the table with a sly grin creeping across her face. "You thought he and I were a thing."

"No, I did not."

"Oh, damn. You did. Delarosa is jealous."

"Sit down."

She slid in the booth as Katie walked in the front, locking the door behind her. We were not scheduled to open for another thirty minutes. "Who was the guy I passed and why was the door unlocked?"

"Nick Villano, DEA agent and pilot. Teaching us all about flying aircraft under the radar," Monica said.

"And I missed him? Damn, he is one tree I'd like to climb."

"You and me both, but he's married."

"Down to business, please? Lamar Shanks?" I said, killing the lustful drool of the Nick Villano fan club.

"Married? Figures." Katie opened her laptop computer on the table. "What about before he was married? The two of you?"

"How about you and I dish later. Johnny is jealous, and we don't want to further upset him," Monica jabbed.

"No kidding?" Katie was eager to take full advantage and pounce. "I didn't take you for the jealous type."

"Sit down. Shanks?" I said, not able to hide my chagrin.

"Struck a nerve, Mons. Interesting. Maybe I should threaten to call Leah. Work my own blackmail scheme?"

"I'll split it with you." They slapped a high five.

"Are you two finished? Shanks and DeRenzo, please."

"Mons, are we?"

"For now."

They both worked last night on background information on Lamar Shanks after Dee Dee gave up his name as a credible Kenzie accomplice. If he connected to the blackmail, my goal was to end it now.

Monica pulled a sheet of paper from her jacket pocket. "Lamar Jerome Shanks. Thirty-three years old. Did two years in Janesville for possession and distribution. Still on parole and his PO says he is clean and current with parole requirements. Works building maintenance for Port City Community College. Address is an apartment in Fulton."

"Nothing to add. No military background to connect him to Anthony. Remember, we never got an address for Kenzie. If he was her dealer, it must have been a few years ago," Katie said.

"Monica, when did he come out of Janesville?"

"Year and a half. Do we check him out?"

"I do. If you go, he'll clam up. I go as a PI helping my client. Katie, our buddy Anthony. Address?"

"Townhouse in Wentworth. He drove there after the terrible fire at his mother's house. Hasn't moved all morning."

"By the way, DeRenzo and Roberto 'Bobby' Rodriguez were honorably discharged from the Army, and both did multiple tours as pilots in the Middle East. Rodriguez was from New York. They probably connected in the service. Also, I checked with the FAA and both are rated for instruments and twin-engine aircraft," Monica added.

"Which means they have the expertise to pull off a low-altitude night flight." I slipped out of the booth. "Text me Lamar's address. Monica, we'll call you if Anthony moves. And by the way, the muscles, flat stomach, and the tattoos are all compensation for being lousy in bed."

"Sure," Monica said. "Keep telling yourself that."

36

The address for Lamar Shanks was in Fulton, an older, worn-out section of the city. Garden style apartment buildings with bars on the first-floor windows were commonplace. Lamar's was no different. Each building had a glass front door. Beside the door was a directory with unit numbers and names and a button to press. I thought announcing myself was not the smartest move, so I yanked on the door and it opened. So much for security in a high-crime area.

Shanks was one flight up in 2B. From inside the apartment, a game show blared from a television. I knocked. The volume lowered, the locks clicked, and the door cracked open, pulling the safety chain taut. An African American man peered at me.

"Hey, is Lamar in? Name is Delarosa."

"Not here." The door slammed shut and the TV volume went back up.

I knocked hard and said through the door, "I'm a private detective, and only want to ask a couple questions about a mutual friend."

The door opened again, the chain drawing tight. The same man. "I highly doubt me and you have a mutual friend."

"Kenzie Fitzgerald. I'm not the police, only want a minute. Please." I held up my investigator's license. "A minute."

"Already talked to the cops 'bout that."

"You did? Who? A detective? Shit, those bastards. They accuse you of anything?"

He stared at me through the opening, his eyes running me up and down. The door closed, the chain slid, and he opened it, nodding for me to go in. I did and walked into a wall of acrid smoke hanging in the air. One way to start your day—smoking weed with the *Price is Right*. I thought I would be buzzed just by standing there.

Shanks was skinny, in his thirties, with short dreads, a white wife-beater T-shirt, baggy jeans, and three gold chains around his neck. He disappeared into the kitchen, came back and handed me a business card. *Paul Ellison*.

"When was he here?" *Damn, he was a good detective.*

"Other day."

"He ask how you knew Kenzie?"

"Yeah."

"What did you say?"

"From back in the day."

"He ask about how she got killed?" He nodded. "And?"

"Like I told him, I don't know nothing about that or her life. Haven't seen her since I got out. I'm keeping cool, doing my thing. On parole, with no intention of going back inside."

The apartment had an L-shaped living and dining area with only a sofa, the television on a stand, and a small table. Nothing in the dining room, no pictures on the walls. If he had money, it certainly was not spent on interior decorating.

"I understand. But how did Detective Ellison link you to Kenzie?"

"Hell if I know. That it?"

"No, because I am now your best friend."

"Shit."

"I said I am a private investigator, but my concern is not Kenzie Fitzgerald. My concern is Stan Shelton."

"Who?"

"The car dealer, old NFL quarterback. Every other commercial on TV."

He shrugged. "So?"

"He's my client. And I believe Kenzie was running a play against him, trying to jack him up for cash."

"What's that got to do with me?"

"You tell me. Ellison had your name and now I do. Why? Someone is giving you up as her partner in the blackmail scam. Kenzie put you up to making the phone call for a nice payday. Then she gets dead and here you are, in your shitty apartment, so you decide to call Stan again, on your own. Am I getting warm?"

"Hell, no, dude. You need to go."

"What, you don't want to find out why I am your best friend?"

He opened the door. "I got to go to work."

"Detective Ellison is dead. And he took all his notes with him. The only person who can connect you to Kenzie is me, and whoever is handing out your name like candy."

He closed the door. "Dead?" His eyes were wide.

"Yep, found him floating in the old quarry."

"Dang. Hey, nothing to do with me. Man, I can't have any cops coming around to jam me up on a murder thing."

"All between you and me now. Here's the deal. Stop the blackmail calls, and I lose your name. All my client wants is for this to go away. So, take it from the top. Kenzie contacts you, tells you about a guy who is loaded, all you need to do is make the call to Stan..."

"Ridiculous, man. How do I trust you?"

"My client is worried his name will be leaked if the cops are involved. You stop calling, it all disappears."

"Wait, what are you talking about? Stop calling? I only called one time."

"Once?" We stared at each other for a second. "Tell me what happened."

"Shit, man, if this goes bad, I will do some damage on somebody." He paced around in a small circle. "Kenzie shows up here one night. I figure she wants to get high, but I tell her I'm not dealing anymore. Trying to get my life straight, know what I'm sayin'?"

I waved my hand through the haze hanging from the ceiling.

"Nah, man, she went hard. So, she tells me about this other deal. A rich dude, and a shot for some cash. I agreed, made the call, then nothing. I don't hear from her. I reached out, nothing. I figured I got played and it went down without me. Then I see her on the news. I swear, that's it."

"You only called once?"

"Yeah. One time, now she's dead and I got cops up in my shit."

I believed him. Not sure why, but he certainly did not seem to be the type to possess the business acumen to open an offshore bank account in the Cayman Islands. I handed him my card. "Anyone else comes around, keep your mouth shut, except to call me. You got my word; your name stays with me."

"I ain't going back to Janesville for making a call to some dude."

"Don't blame you. Trust me."

I opened the door and stepped out, happy to leave the hanging marijuana haze and breathe the putrid, urine-tainted air in the stairwell.

He stood in the apartment doorway. "She was a fine ass white chick. She never had any money, so we worked out an arrangement. Partied and such."

"I can only imagine. I bet you miss her."

"Man, I'm in mourning."

My phone buzzed as I got to my car. A message from Katie:

"Anthony's car headed to Davis."

"Okay, tell Monica. I'm coming in."

If Lamar only made the first call, who made the subsequent demands? Anthony? Was he in on the blackmail from the beginning? And was Lamar their scapegoat in case the scheme backfired? Dee Dee had given me Lamar's name. With Kenzie dead, how did Paul Ellison link her to Lamar?

37

My second text from Katie came through as soon as I turned on to the highway. Stan's car was also headed to Davis Airfield. I jumped off at the next exit, and pulled into a gas station and called her.

"I am going to the airfield. Stan has me curious."

"Pick me up."

"No, stay on the computer. Text with any changes."

I ended the call amid her loud protest and opened the maps app on my smartphone, deeply pleased with myself that I learned how to operate the phone. The airfield was on Parish Road, south of Port City, five miles inland from the ocean. A quarter-mile prior to the airfield was Old Church Road, which ran east-west, parallel to the runway, and now my destination.

Thirty minutes later, I first drove past the airfield to check the parking lot. The black Jeep Cherokee and a blue Corvette were side by side. I turned around in a driveway and doubled back and turned left on Old Church, putting a corn field between me and the runway.

After a few hundred yards, I pulled to the shoulder and hoped I was isolated enough that my car would not draw suspicion. I grabbed my camera, the 300 mm lens, and a pair of binoculars from the trunk and headed into the six-foot-tall stalks of summer.

I trudged through the field, staying between corn rows, ducking when the stalks were short, and arrived at the edge of the field, where the corn provided the perfect cover. I took a supine position and the long camera lens brought me to the tarmac, with the small terminal building in the background. Two men walked around the twin-engine Beechcraft in an apparent pre-flight inspection. I easily identified Anthony DeRenzo and assumed the second man was Rodriguez, and snapped off several decent shots of his face and the call numbers stenciled on the tail rudder.

Not two minutes later, the booming voice of Stan Shelton carried across the runway. He had come out of the terminal wearing the most god-awful yellow pastel pants and a white golf shirt. He gathered the men in a huddle. The fact both pilots conducted a pre-flight check of the aircraft was meaningless, but with Stan added to the mix, it meant everything. Was he a willing participant of the alleged trafficking of young girls through Port City on their way to New York, or were Anthony and Talia keeping him in the dark?

The two pilots boarded the plane, started the engines, and taxied to the far end of the runway. The propellers roared as the Beechcraft rolled along the black strip, eventually lifting into the air, climbing in altitude, and disappearing as a shrinking dot in the sky.

For a moment, I thought about the beautiful the sight of this man-made machine taking flight, until I remembered its vile mission. Shelton remained on the tarmac with a phone pressed to his ear. I photographed it all.

He went inside the building and I decided I had seen enough. DeRenzo and Rodriguez leaving on a sunny afternoon proved nothing, but them returning under the cover of darkness with a full-complement of illegals would prove everything.

I emerged from the maze of corn to find a man sitting on the hood of my BMW. He spotted me and hopped off. Not a tall man, but the shotgun in his arms made up for his lack of height. He wore overalls, a blue T-shirt, a John Deere ball cap, and had a long white beard.

"Now, exactly what can I help you with?" He leveled the weapon at my chest.

I raised my hands, camera in one, binoculars in the other. "Nothing. Name's Delarosa. I'm a private detective."

"Really, now. And you are investigating, what? Insects on my corn? What did you find? Aphids? Beetles?"

"I was tracking a few men at the airport and your field here made for a perfect vantage point. Didn't mean to trespass. No harm done."

A pickup truck traveled down Old Church toward us and stopped behind my car. The driver's door opened and a man hopped out. Bill Davis from the airfield, with a striking resemblance to the man holding the shotgun.

"What the hell is going on here?" he said.

Mister Shotgun responded, "This man says he's a private detective investigating something at the airfield."

Bill Davis came a little closer. "Hey, you're the fella from the other day. You came in with your wife."

Hoo boy. This could work in my favor, or, on the off-chance Bill Davis was a partner in the trafficking operation, this could be very bad for my health. I remembered how Nick Villano said Bill Davis was a great guy.

"Yes, Mister Davis. Sorry about the other day, and not being truthful with you, but the woman who was with me is Detective Mattson with the PCPD. We were working a case that unfortunately could involve one of your pilots."

"You mean the good-looking gal with the freckles? She's a detective?"

"Yes."

"I'll be damned. What kind of case?"

"Rather not say."

"You'd rather not say? Well, this here is my brother Jacob, and you are on his farm. And the twelve gauge in his hand is kindly asking you to tell us what you're investigating."

A reasonable request if I ever heard one. So I did, taking the gamble that Davis could be complicit in the nefarious activity. If he was, then I was soon to be fertilizer in the field. I explained how we suspected Anthony DeRenzo, and possibly Rodriguez, were using Stan Shelton's plane to bring girls through this area on their way to New York.

After what I thought was going to be a staring contest ending in a shotgun blast, Jacob finally said, "Shelton always was a bullshitter."

"You're saying they're flying in here at night with illegals from South America?" Bill asked. "Sounds far-fetched to me."

"It does, but Nick Villano can vouch for me. I met with him, and he said you were his instructor. We can contact him."

"Nick?" He paused for a moment, took a cell phone from his pocket and made a call. After a second: "Hey, Nick? Bill Davis." He walked away, out of earshot. A minute later, the phone was back in his pocket. "Put the gun down, Jacob," he said. "Explains a lot."

"How so?" I asked.

"Fuel usage I couldn't account for, canceled flight lessons because they said Stan had them flying all night. They would always blame it on him being spontaneous. Like today."

"Where were they going?"

"Shelton wanted them to pick up a buddy in North Carolina and bring him back here. I noticed they didn't file a flight plan, and when I said something, they brushed me off."

"Stan Shelton has himself surrounded by some nasty people. I'm not sure he is aware of how nasty. The FBI is involved. I stumbled into this by accident. My advice to you is to keep it business as usual."

"If these people are up to no good, we want to help. We don't want nothing illegal on our property," said Jacob.

"Yeah, he's right. What can we do?" Bill added.

"Fair enough. Watch out for anything unusual. Like the flight plan today. But most important, keep all this to yourself."

"I had a pilot buddy who worked for the Texas Border Patrol, and he would tell me all these crazy stories of how the cartels would smuggle in drugs, weapons, and people. I figured it was a Texas problem."

"Unfortunately, no. Once they get the contraband—people, in this case—into the country, then they need to move them around without being detected."

"Sex trafficking?" Jacob said.

"Human trafficking. Some are put to work as prostitutes, some are coerced into domestic servitude. Forced labor."

Jacob shook his head. "Not using our land for that kind of nonsense."

"Alleged, don't forget. I don't blame you, but if either of your pilots suspects anything, they could move the operation elsewhere. And they'll take care of any loose ends. And guess who the loose ends are?" I pointed at the two of them.

"Like hell." Jacob scoffed.

"Please maintain your everyday routines. If all this is true, our best chance is to catch them in the act. Bill, put my number in your phone." I recited my number as he punched it in. "Text me if you see anything odd, but please, don't confront them. Send me a message if they come back before you leave at the end of the day. The FBI suspects they are moving girls in the next few days. Tonight could be the night."

"Will do," Bill said. "If they are running underage girls and using my airfield, promise me one crack at them. Just one."

"We'd all love a shot, but we need to let law enforcement handle it." I shook hands with the brothers. "I do have one question. The lights on the runway, do they come on automatically at night?"

"No. When the pilot is approaching, say anywhere within five to ten miles out, he tunes to the airfield's radio frequency and clicks the mic three times and the lights come on," Bill explained.

"Fascinating," I said.

I thank them and we agreed to stay in touch. Jacob got in Bill's truck and they rumbled off. I turned my BMW around and headed for the city, worried I created two potential loose ends for Talia to snip.

38

While bargaining for my future with Bill and Jacob Davis, I missed four text messages on my phone. A few miles from the airfield, I turned the BMW in to a convenience store lot. The first message was from Dee Dee telling me Talia agreed to meet and to be at the same location on Rosewood at 9:00 p.m. Surprised, I thanked her with a response. The next three were from Katie asking me to call.

She picked up on the first ring. "Where are you?"

"Leaving Davis Airfield, on my way in."

"Please hurry. Stan Shelton is here, drinking and telling stories to anyone who will listen. So obnoxious. And if he grabs my ass one more time, I am going to stab him with a fork."

"No stabbing. I will be there in thirty."

I placed a call to Gil Evans, the FBI special agent heading the investigation. His voice mail came on and I left a message, telling him the Beechcraft had just left Davis. They could be picking up Stan's friend in North Carolina, or not.

Several thoughts collided in my head as I drove back to the city. The first was the Davis brothers. Holding them in my confidence could work to my advantage but having to explain the entire operation to two good old boys made me nervous. The last thing I needed were shotgun vigilantes waiting for the plane to land. I hoped Nick Villano told Bill to trust me and to stay out of the way.

The second was Stan. He was at the airfield not thirty minutes ago and now he was at McNally's, preaching to his faithful in the middle of the day? Why? And his hand on Katie's ass irked me. I hoped she did stab him.

He was in full Stan-the-man mode when I walked in, at a table with two girls in his lap and three guys gathered around, all enthralled in another tall tale of his football glory days.

"See," Katie said.

"You two, up," I said to the girls. "C'mon, Stan, we need to talk." I pulled him from the chair.

"Damn, Johnny." He adjusted the front of his awful yellow pants as he stood. "I just can't pop up like that. What do you think happens when two women are sitting in your lap?"

"It will go down."

One of the guys from the table came after us. "Hey, man, leave him alone."

"Shut up. I own the place. Go back to your seat. Next round is on me."

"I can pay for my own drinks, and if Stan Shelton wants to sit with us, he can," the kid protested.

"I said, go back to your seat."

Mike walked in and immediately sensed the ruckus. His presence alone brought an instant calm. He stared the kid back to his table without saying a word.

I pushed Stan into my booth. "What are you doing?"

"Celebrating. It's over. I came here to tell you."

"What is over?"

"Everything—the blackmail, the threat of exposing me. Thank you for helping me the way you did. I appreciate it. And I'm serious, this place is my new place. I am going to bring you so much business, you'll need to hire more girls. Please make sure they are as fine as my Katie. Where is she, anyhow? She should be here to celebrate. That girl does something to me." He winked and pulled a checkbook from his pocket. "How much do I owe?"

"What the hell are you talking about? What did you do?"

He cocked his head and spoke with a newfound confidence. "Ended it. I know you might be mad, because you told me to do nothing, but it ate away at my insides. I couldn't sleep, work, nothing. I'm sorry, but I completed the deal and transferred the money. I figured out a way that Nikki would not find out. Johnny, I can breathe again."

All I could do was stare in disbelief. My brain immediately kicked back to his history—lying, cheating, scheming, always working his way out of a jam he brought on himself. Jacob Davis's words rang in my head: *"Shelton always was a bullshitter."*

"Johnny, what do I owe you? And I am adding a bonus for Katie."

"Come with me." I slid out of the booth.

He hesitated.

"C'mon."

He stood; I grabbed his arm and pulled him into the kitchen and through the back door into the alley. He had two inches on me and a solid forty pounds, but my anger and adrenaline took over. I pushed him against the brick wall of the building.

"Hey, what the hell?"

I got inches from his face. "Two people are dead. Do you realize that? Neither one would have died if you had the ability to control your behavior, and now I think you lied to me this entire time. Who made the phone calls? Who came to your office?"

"I don't know what you are talking about."

Katie appeared in the alley. "Johnny."

"Go back inside," I yelled. She ran in.

"Stan, you need to come clean now. Why did you transfer the money? And to where? Grand Caymans? And where is your plane headed right now?"

"My plane?"

"You thought I wouldn't discover you're transporting girls into Port City?"

"What? Girls? I sent them to pick up a friend of mine."

I slammed him against the building again. "Tell me the truth, Stan."

"Get the hell off." He shoved me back. "Do not make me hit you, John."

My fist landed first, a hard right to the side of his face, and he went down to the pavement. "That is for Paul Ellison."

Mike and Katie burst out to the alley.

"The drunk detective who fell in the quarry? He was a lush," he said.

I drew back my fist again but Mike got between us. "Hold up, hold up."

"You son-of-a-bitch, Shelton," I said. "You will not weasel out of this the way you do everything else."

Mike pulled Stan to his feet and pointed at me. "Be smart."

"Goddamn, Johnny. We are done. I'll mail you a check."

"Like hell. Up to my place, now. You are not leaving until we sort all this out. Katie, take him upstairs and wait until I get there."

She reached out to take his arm, but he shook her off and walked to the stairs, where she followed him up.

"You okay?" Mike asked.

"Nothing fazes him. Two dead, and all is good? Unreal. I might need your help later. We can't let him out of our sight."

"Anything."

"I'm sure I'll pay for this somehow."

"Hey, he deserved to be punched for wearing the yellow pants."

39

"Start explaining or I turn you over to the police," I said, backing Stan against the refrigerator in my kitchen.

"Police? For what? Escort services are legal."

"How about the illegal trafficking of underage girls? Wait till the press sinks their teeth into that story. Famous quarterback pays for teenage girls to come into the country to work as prostitutes."

His brow furrowed. "What are you talking about? You said that downstairs."

"You need to come clean now. Start from the top." I pulled out a kitchen chair. "Sit."

He did, and I poured him a Scotch against my better judgment, but I needed to grease him a bit. He had to tell me everything or I would push him off the quarry cliff myself.

"I already told you everything."

"No. Dee Dee. You hired her, and—"

"John, I'm sorry I got you mixed up in all this. Can we call it a day? We're good now. And the stuff about young girls sounds sick and nasty. Not my thing. Today is a great day and we should celebrate."

I leaned against the kitchen counter. *This man was seriously delusional about reality.* As a sports celebrity, he must have been so insulated from the consequences of his actions that he now believed he could solve anything with money and bullshit. The NFL protected him when he gambled on games, and God only knows how many times his wives ignored the skirt-chasing in exchange for the lifestyle. But I was determined.

I slammed a chair into the table and got in his face. "Now. Stan. I want the truth. Did you forget about Kenzie and Detective Ellison? They are dead because of your actions. You okay with that? All is good, why? Because you paid off some scumbags? You need to decide on which side of the bars you want to spend the rest of your days. And I'm not talking about bars that serve drinks. Start with Dee Dee."

He stared at the table for a minute. Then leaned back in the chair with his eyes closed.

"Stan, I am your only friend, whether you like it or not. You need to believe me, because this is going to go sideways, very fast. And it will not be some celebrity sex scandal where you are crying and contrite and go to some phony rehab for sex addiction. Think about life in prison for a football star. They'll bend you over like you're the center, but it won't be their hands they stick under your ass. Those dudes will pay each other for a turn with you. You'll be the Super Bowl trophy."

"Is that supposed to be funny?"

"No, not at all." I walked to my balcony door and talked with my back to him. "Second thought, you are right—it is over. I'm done. You can go to hell." I turned around. "Tell your story to the FBI."

"Okay, okay. I'm sorry." He sat forward, elbows on the table, head in his hands. "I hired Dee Dee. Picked her out from the website. We had a couple of dates and I liked her. We hit it off. All that is true. After the fifth or sixth date, she tells me the owner of the company wants to meet with me. To talk business. Sounded intriguing, so I agreed and met with Talia. You know who I am talking about?"

I nodded. "Where did you meet?"

"At my loft. Incredible woman. I can't even describe her. Has these eyes that are some wild shade of green I've never seen before."

"I'm familiar."

"She asked me to invest, said she wanted to expand the business. Wanted me to partner with her and said there was a lot of money to be made. I said I would think about it and one hour later, two incredible girls show up at the loft and we, umm, closed the deal. I agreed to invest a million. Two separate transfers. I told Talia I couldn't transfer all the money at once."

"Kenzie?"

"Two weeks after I made the first transfer was when Kenzie showed up at the dealership, threatening to expose me."

"Did you tell Talia?"

"Yes. She listened, said to not worry about it. I told Dee Dee, and she reassured me Kenzie had nothing to do with the company and was working her own scam. Told me to not pay her. But I was so impatient, scared, I couldn't help it and came to see you. Did not want my name to get out. Dee Dee was furious with me for hiring you."

He emptied his glass and I refilled it. "Keep going."

"Kenzie was killed. You said it was a message killing, and I knew instantly the message was for me. That the blackmail threat was over. But I didn't want to admit to you my involvement with the company."

"Who killed her?"

He stretched his body in the seat, rolled his head around. Let out a long sigh. "I figured Talia. Stopping the blackmail."

"You talked to her after Kenzie was killed?"

"No. I asked Dee Dee to arrange a call, but it didn't happen."

"So, the other two calls had nothing to do with Kenzie?"

"No, they were about the money I owed to Talia. I was late in paying, mostly because the Kenzie thing had me freaked out."

"The trafficking? What do you know?"

He sat forward and stared me dead in the eye. "Nothing. I swear, Johnny. I don't know what you are talking about."

My phone vibrated. The screen displayed, Gil Evans. "Do not move," I said to Stan and went to my balcony to take the call. "Agent Evans," I answered.

"Delarosa, thanks for the info on the plane. Good work. We just got word the girls are on the move, we think headed to an airstrip near Canton, Georgia. North of Atlanta."

"How can I help?"

"You already did, but I wouldn't mind eyes on the airfield. I tried Detective Mattson. Left four messages. She with you?"

"No, haven't seen her today."

"Keep trying, if you wouldn't mind. I will, too. Keep me posted."

"Will do."

I ended the call with Evans and tried Monica's phone. Her voicemail came on, I left a message asking her to call me.

Back inside, I thought, *Decision time for me. How much do I divulge?* I could hold back, but it was come-to-Jesus time for Stan. My smartest move would be to gauge his reaction.

"The FBI suspects Talia is complicit in the trafficking of young girls from South America, flying them into Port City on their way to New York. Are you saying you have no knowledge of your plane being used to fly girls up the coast?"

"Hell no. For God's sake. I'm not perfect by any means, but there is no way I would be involved in that." He stood and moved away from the table as if I were contagious. "The young girl stuff is deplorable. You got to believe me."

"Your plane, today. Where was it going?"

"North Carolina. Pick up a friend."

"Who?"

"My friend? Jimmy Trimble. You remember him, played for Minnesota. Coming up to play golf for a few days."

"Can DeRenzo and Rodriguez access your plane without your approval?"

"Yes, I allow them to use it whenever they want. Part of a deal I have with them..." He trailed off, I'm certain realizing the two pilots could be using his airplane without his knowledge.

"I want you to look me in the eye and tell me the truth. You know nothing about sex trafficking and flying girls from the south to here?"

"Johnny, are you nuts? Please, please, believe me. I would lose everything."

"I want to believe you." My voice went up an octave. "I do. But if you are not telling me the truth, I will march you to the FBI myself. After I shoot you."

He threw up his hands. "Fair enough. I don't want my name—or my airplane—or my pilots, associated with any of that kind...of stuff. You think Talia is involved? If so, I'll pay you extra to keep me out of this."

"The FBI thinks she is. What I can do is keep you tucked away and out of sight. Every time I say go home and stay there, you take off. You need to distance yourself from these people, especially now. Including Dee Dee."

"Johnny..."

"Including Dee Dee. The FBI is all over this. Call Nikki and make something up. Sleep here tonight."

"What do I tell her? I will go home and lock the doors. I swear."

"Non-negotiable. Actually, I have a better idea. How would you like to spend the night with Katie?"

"Huh?" His eyebrows went up and his eyes widened. He dug into a pocket. "Where's my phone? Calling Nikki now."

40

"Seriously?" she asked, loud enough to turn patrons' heads.

"Lower your voice." Katie and I stood next to my booth at the rear of McNally's when I detailed my plan for her to baby sit Stan at my beach place overnight. "We'll load him up with booze and he'll sleep."

"Where is he now?" Her arms were folded across her chest.

"Upstairs, stretched out on my sofa."

"You lost your mind if you think I am going to spend a second with that perv. I'll be black and blue from fighting him off."

I pulled her into the booth and explained that Stan's plane took off earlier and how Gil Evans said the girls were on the move, most likely headed to an airfield. "This is going down tonight. Please do this. I'm betting the plane comes back with girls, and I need to keep Stan where we can watch him. He denies knowing about the trafficking, but I don't know what to believe with him."

"He's lying."

"We don't know."

"I do. He's a perverted dirty old man." She shook her head. "I am not sitting all night at the beach house unless you give me a gun. I'll shoot him if he comes near me. Give me an instant lesson, right now."

"I promise I will take you to the range, and I will give you a gun for tonight. You need to have protection, but please don't shoot Stan."

"No promises."

"Did Monica call you?"

"No, why?"

"Evans can't reach her. I tried, too. No luck."

Katie tapped Monica's name on her phone, and it clicked immediately to voice mail. "Should we call Captain Lane?"

"Not yet. I'll keep trying. Take your car to the beach, then hide the key in my toolbox. I don't want to give him a way to escape."

She smirked. "I'll put sleeping pills in his Scotch."

"Don't do that either." I grabbed her hand. "Thank you. Make sure your phone is charged. Stop for some food on your way out. Call me if you sense anything suspicious. Anything at all. You have your emergency bag of clothes?"

"Of course." We got up from the booth. "Johnny?" She hesitated for a second. "Should I be scared?"

"Probably, but nobody knows about the beach house but you." I took her hand again. "If you are not up to this, please decide now."

"No, I'm fine. I'll do it."

"Okay, come upstairs as soon as you can."

The Beretta .22 and shells were on the top shelf of my bedroom closet. I heard Stan stir in the front room as I loaded the gun. If she did shoot him, the small caliber might not kill him, but would definitely scare him, or anyone else. I put it on my dresser and went to the living room.

"C'mon, Stan. Time to go."

He roused from the sofa and helped himself to a beer from the fridge. "What's the plan?"

"You and Katie are going to stay hidden away tonight. I am trusting you on the trafficking, but the deal is you keep out of sight. Cool?"

"Damn, Johnny. What guy wouldn't want to spend a night hidden away with Blondie?"

"Let's set something straight. She has permission to shoot you if you even look at her the wrong way. Keep your distance. Got it?"

"Hell, yes, I'm only kidding. Why are we doing this again?"

"Got word about something tonight and I want you tucked away. Out of the line of fire."

"Should I be nervous about this?"

"Very. And give me your phone."

"Hell, no."

"Hell, yes." My phone rang. Davis Aviation appeared on the screen. "Be right back." I stepped out to the balcony and closed the sliding door. "Delarosa."

"Bill Davis here, calling to tell you the Beechcraft is back."

"Stan's plane?"

"Yep. I went out for a bit and when I got back, there it was."

"Was that enough time for them to fly to North Carolina and back?"

"Not really. Must have changed their plans. False alarm, huh?"

"Appears so. The pilots still around?"

"Nope, only me and I'm about to lock up."

"Well, thanks for the call. I appreciate it."

"Anytime. Happy to help."

I clicked off. The plane was back—why the change? Something told me to keep that information to myself for the moment. Stan didn't tell me the truth from the start. He was not honest with me about the phone calls and his involvement with Talia—why should I believe him now about the trafficking?

Katie and Stan were in the kitchen, discussing football, when I went in. Their conversation seemed normal and civil, so I took it as a positive sign.

I had her follow me into the bedroom where I demonstrated the gun. "This is a Beretta .22. It is loaded, easy to use—here is the safety. Click it off, point, and squeeze the trigger. If anything would happen, somebody comes out there, make sure you identify your target. I don't want you to shoot me. And you only shoot as a last resort."

"Got it, boss. What about more ammo?"

"More ammo? If you need more bullets, then we are in big trouble."

"Just want to be prepared." She put the gun in her purse.

"You have plenty. Let's go." We went to the kitchen. "Stan, phone." I held out my hand.

"Johnny, please."

"Only way, Stan. Or I throw you to the wolves."

He handed me his phone. "Boy," he said to Katie. "Your boss here is no joke."

"Either am I," she said.

"And I thought this was going to be a fun night." He winked.

"She'll drive her car. Katie, text me when you get to the beach. Lock the doors."

"Copy that, chief."

"Stan, behave."

"Copy that, chief," he said.

And out they went, with me hoping to God I called the right play.

41

A three-quarter moon peeked over the horizon to begin its trek across the sky on a clear but humid night. It was 8:00 p.m., one hour before my meeting with Talia. I wore a white shirt, jeans, and laid out my blue blazer. Katie sent a text confirming their arrival at the beach cottage. So far, so good. I poured a short bourbon and took it to the chaise lounge on my balcony. A dramatic sunset of yellow and orange shapes and layers filled my view and I thought the perverse actions of tonight were such a contrast to God's beauty on display.

I tried Gil Evans again, my third call in the past hour; the first two went to his voice mail. He answered after two rings. "Delarosa, glad you called back."

"Wanted you to know the plane is at Davis Airfield. Didn't go to Georgia after all."

"What? How do you know? Our agent on site confirmed four girls boarding a twin-engine Beechcraft."

"My man at the airstrip told me it came back early."

He paused; a shuffling of papers. "Are we talking the same aircraft? Any chance you took pictures of the call letters?"

"Sure did. Hold on." I went inside, set the phone on my kitchen table, pulled my camera from the case and scrolled through the shots I took from the cornfield. I stopped on a picture with a clear view of the rudder and zoomed in.

"Evans?"

"Go ahead."

"The numbers are N3123Z."

"Yep, matches the plane in Georgia. Took off an hour ago."

My stomach dropped. The same plane. Bill Davis lied to me, which means he, and probably his brother Jacob, were part of team Talia.

"Obviously I received bad info. We'll get out to the airfield."

"Remember, please observe. We want intelligence on all the players in the chain. If we disrupt the line now, it could blow the entire investigation."

"Understood."

"Hey, any word from Mattson?"

"None. Has me concerned."

"I have my phone beside me all night. Don't hesitate."

"Will do."

I slipped my phone into my pocket and stood in the middle of my kitchen. This case had been a series of lies from the start. Stan never told the truth, whether it was about Kenzie, the phone calls, his financial involvement with Talia, or his airplane going for his friend. A professional bullshitter to begin with, I was disappointed in myself for allowing him any benefit of the doubt. And now, a lie from the Davis brothers, who had to be links in the chain.

Somehow, though, after all the deceit, I still wondered whether Stan was the ultimate mark. Did they use his plane without his knowledge? It was possible. Did Talia entice him with women, promise him money, have Dee Dee satisfy his every need, just to boost him up to the legend in his own mind? He had an ego the size of a football field, and she did a hall-of-fame job of keeping it fed.

If Anthony DeRenzo and Bobby Rodriguez were flying girls to Port City tonight, and we could confront Stan with their actions, the night could finally reveal the truth.

The bourbon went down smooth, but I refrained from a second pour. I needed to keep a clear head if I was to match wits with Talia. I slipped on my shoulder holster with my Beretta, grabbed my blazer and went downstairs.

"You got a date?" Mike said, as he set two beers on the bar.

"Something like that. What's this?"

"They won their championship."

A bowling team and their groupies filled the place and their celebration was in full swing.

"Damn. I planned on you for back up tonight."

"On my own, here, brother. Carlos pulled overtime. I'll kick them out as soon as I can, but they are in a happy mood and the money is loose." Two bowlers, with *The*

Gutter Ballers, emblazoned on the back of their shirts, staggered to the bar and ordered shots for everyone.

"Text me when you close up," I said. "Sorry to leave you."

"Nothing I can't handle."

###

The address on Rosewood was the same spot I met Anthony the first time I had a meeting with Talia. It was 8:50 p.m., ten minutes early, so I tried Monica again. Nothing. It immediately went to voice mail, as if the phone were off.

Katie and Stan were safely at the beach house. Mike's hands were full at McNally's. The lack of contact from Monica worried me. Even if she was working and not in a position to answer her phone, she would at least send a message. A check of my gut told me Bill Davis lied, the plane was on its way to Port City, and Monica was in jeopardy. How, why, and where was the mystery.

The German-made digital clock in the dashboard of my BMW Z-4 clicked to 9:00 as a black Jeep Cherokee with black rims turned in to the parking lot. Anthony? He was to be flying the illegal aliens from Atlanta to Davis Airfield.

The car stopped beside me and the driver's window went down. *Dee Dee.*

Surprised, but not shocked, I lowered my window.

"Change of plans," she said.

"I don't like change."

"Meet Talia at Max's. She's waiting."

"Hey, not even a hello?"

"You blew your chance." She squealed out of the lot and disappeared.

I started the engine and headed for Max's, curious as hell as to what truth the night had in store.

42

The first oddity was the vacant street in front of Max's. The bar would normally be open at this hour. I parked my car at the curb and got out. The second was the sidewalks were empty, as if it were Super Bowl Sunday and everyone was home watching the game. A placard on the door: Closed for a Private Event. My first, albeit scary, thought was Talia planned a private party and I was the only guest. I pulled open the door and the second thought was a snare waited inside and I would never be seen again.

Talia sat at the end of the bar. Alone. No bartender, no other patrons. She wore jeans, a black T-shirt, and ankle boots. Her hair was down and around her like a protective shield. She smiled as I approached.

"I figured you had some power, but the place all to ourselves?" I said.

"Cozy, don't you think?" Her hand was wrapped around a martini. "Drink?"

"Of course." I pointed to hers. "One of those." I took the stool beside her.

She hopped off hers and walked behind the bar.

"Bartender, too?"

"I make a killer martini."

I glanced around for thugs lurking in the corners. None. "Gin or vodka?" I asked.

"Gin. The only way to go."

She made the drink—stirred, not shaken—and put the glass in front of me, then came around and took her seat. "To dark yesterdays and bright tomorrows," she said, as we raised our glasses.

I gazed into her siren eyes.

But she had these vivid, emerald eyes and I couldn't stop staring. Eyes that belonged on the cover of a magazine, not hidden in the obscenity of a crack-house hotel.

"They have always been my strong suit. Men love them," she said, as if she read my thoughts.

I did a slow nod, taking in her face, the hair, all of her. "I appreciate the privacy tonight. Not sure how you pulled it off, but impressive."

"I thought you would. What's on your mind? Besides me."

I smiled. "Only you." I sipped the martini. "Perfect." I set the drink on the bar. "Not to ruin the moment, but we need to talk."

"A moment? Sounds like you're going to ruin another night."

"I'm disappointed in your line of work."

"Escort business?" Our legs touched and she leaned in close. "Nothing wrong in providing a needed service. Right?"

I half-whispered, "Let's not waste time. The other line of work." Even though I requested the meeting, I wondered what her goal was for tonight.

"You mean the one where I take girls and give them a life they could never imagine growing up in some God-forsaken third world country."

I nodded.

"With me, they have a chance. A chance to succeed, make real money, buy food, a clean place to live, nice clothes, help their families," she said.

"It doesn't justify the means. They are illegal. What you are doing is illegal. They will eventually be sent back and you'll be arrested."

"You don't really believe that, do you, Johnny?" She took a serious tone, pulled her hair back so it was off her face.

"Sure I do. How many of those girls end up on the street, like you did? How many will die of overdoses?"

"None. I stay with my girls. I tend to their well-being. They are never alone."

"Remember the damage done to you? They destroyed you, and I am amazed you are sitting here today. Not many girls, women, have the fortitude you had to pull yourself from the dregs of hell and carve out a life. These girls are young, impressionable, limited education, and you are shaping their world. All they will learn is what you teach them."

She stared at her drink while she talked. "Most days, I never think about what happened to me. The childhood I missed, the abuse. You were the only person who helped me and never asked for anything in return." She turned her face to me. "I will never forget your kindness. At the time, I knew you were different, but deep down I thought you wanted what all the others wanted. It wasn't until years later I realized you only had the best of intentions. I am only doing for them what you did for me. In a way, you are responsible."

A *clang* from the kitchen stopped the conversation.

"I thought we were alone," I said.

"Cleaning crew."

"Ah." I scanned around again for thugs in the corners. "I don't want to be responsible for illegal aliens coming into the country to work as prostitutes."

"These girls would find their way to the States eventually. I'm only offering a hand. They appreciate it and remain loyal. I don't want any of them to go through what I went through."

"Talia, I don't know why I did what I did twenty years ago, taking you in. If the department found out, I would have been fired. And I don't know why I am telling you this now, but the FBI is all over this. They're about to close in."

She put her hand on my leg. "Nothing new."

"Not sure I understand..." A sudden queasiness in my stomach... "I can't stop them, and I can't..." A rush of warmth through me. I wiped beads of sweat off my forehead with the back of my hand. "Whoa..."

"Are you okay?"

"Yeah, just felt a little off for a second. Dizzy." Her face blurred and I blinked her back in focus. "I can't stop them..." A tingling in my fingers, arms, legs, traveled through me. "I need some air..." I went down. From the stool to flat on my back on the floor. I gasped... "The drink..."

She crouched beside me, the emerald eyes coming through a curtain of hair. "I told you I make a killer martini." She placed a hand on my chest. "You are a good man, Johnny Delarosa and I will never forget you." Her face came close; I thought she kissed me. "But if you ever get in my way again, I will rain down a hell on you that will make you wish you never saw these green eyes."

43

A cool dampness on my right cheek was the first signal I was alive. *Where was I?* I opened my eyes to blurry darkness as my brain slowly tried to assemble the pieces of my current predicament. Flat on my stomach, a coolness, hands beside my face, my eyes cloudy, but I could breathe. My fingers moved, scratched at...what...the ground, dirt?

I squeezed my eyes closed and sucked in three or four deep breaths hoping they would wake me. *Talia.* She crouched over me. *Talia...*

My eyes opened—and two eyes stared back at me. *What?* Two dark, lifeless eyes. *Was I looking into a mirror?* No. It took a few seconds to register, but I was staring into the eyes of a dead man. The shock jolted me awake and my body reacted with an instinctive jerk to the right to distance myself from him. My right leg dropped out from under me. *Was I falling?*

My hands grasped, clawed at the dirt as my leg dangled beneath me. An edge, a ledge, a what, my body half on the earth, the other half...My heart pounded; my right hand under my chest pressed against the ground to push me from the edge. My left arm flailed, needing to grip...something...only dirt...gravel, in my grasp...nothing to help pull me...If my other leg went off, so would my weight and I'd never be able to hold on...

Finally—my hand touched the arm of the dead man. An anchor. I grabbed his forearm, and he gave new meaning to the term dead weight. I pulled myself from the ledge and rolled against his body. I laid on my back and stared at the stars. My heart pounded; my chest heaved. *Alive.*

The entire ordeal took seconds, but it seemed an eternity. I sat up and looked around. The three-quarter moon on the clear night provided enough light to illuminate a familiar location. The old quarry. They placed me on the edge of the quarry cliff. To die. No, my death left to fate. One roll to my right and I would have dropped into the abyss. I said a prayer to God, every saint, and every dead relative I could think of, thanking them for my life.

I was barefoot. They took my shoes and emptied my pockets. My phone and gun, gone. No car, either. The man, my anchor who saved my life, a very dead Lamar Shanks. *A loose end.* Talia eliminated the loose ends: Kenzie, Paul Ellison, Lamar. But somehow, she left me up to chance. Something stopped her from killing me. If I rolled off the cliff, maybe in her mind it was fate. If I survived, lucky me. *Stan*, I thought—*he was the last loose end.* Would she kill him, too? Or did she need his money? But if he transferred funds like he said, was he now disposable? No, I reminded myself; he and Katie were safe at the beach cottage.

I searched Lamar's pockets. Empty. She was not going to make this easy for me. I struggled to my feet, my head spinning, and found an opening in the rickety snow fence that surrounded the quarry, and gingerly walked across the gravel, realizing I rarely went barefoot. More prayers, this time asking for a car to come along. Anything. I had no idea of the time. The moon was still high, so it had to be around midnight. Talia—she slipped me a mickey to get me out of the way. Did that confirm her transport of girls tonight?

I made it through the parking lot and I got to the road, and nothing. I sat on the pavement and waited. I stopped wearing a watch when I bought a smartphone. With my phone gone, I had no idea of the passing of time. I didn't know whether I waited twenty minutes, or an hour. It sure seemed like an hour. Eventually I laid on my back and stared at the bright moon as it slowly moved across the black sky. Stars shone by the billions and it made me realize my insignificance. How many other beings were in the universe, gazing at these same stars?

Finally, a small vibration on my back. I related to the Indians who could put an ear to the earth and hear horses approaching. I sat up. Headlights appeared in the distance. *Thank God.* I prayed they would stop to help, but I also knew I was about to scare the hell out of the people in the car.

I jumped to the middle of the road and waved my arms. The car slowed, then stopped about thirty yards from me.

"I need help," I yelled. "I am a private investigator and former police officer. Can you help me." I kept my arms above my head and took a few steps toward the car. "Please, I need a ride to Port City."

A female voice screamed, "Turn around and take me home now!"

"Wait, please, I am unarmed." I pulled up my filthy white shirt to show I did not have a weapon. "I'm a private investigator and was drugged and dumped out here. I don't mean to scare you. Can you take me back to the city?"

The car clicked into reverse and began an attempt to turn around on the narrow two-lane road.

"Wait, wait, please." I ran to the driver's window. "Can I at least use a phone? I am stranded out here. My name is John Delarosa, and I am a former detective. I swear." I held my hands in the air.

Two teenagers were in the car, a guy and a girl, obviously headed to the quarry for some quality time in the moonlight.

The girl screamed again, "Tim, take me the fuck home, right now."

"Please, can I use a phone? You can call for me. I'm sorry I scared you, but they took my phone, car, shoes, everything."

The driver's window slid down an inch.

The girl bordered on hysterical. "What are you doing? Let's go, now. He's lying and will fucking kill us. I told you I didn't want to come out here."

"I'm turning the car around," he yelled back.

"I'm begging you, make a call for me. I won't get in. Just make a call, please."

His window went back up, and their voices went back and forth, hers drowning out his. The window opened a crack. "Dude, we need to go. Sorry, man."

"Wait, have your girlfriend make the call. I am a private investigator. I was drugged and dumped out here. Have her call. She'll see I am legit. I co-own a bar in town, McNally's. Please, call my partner."

The window went back up for a second, and then down again. "What's the number?"

"Thank you. His name is Mike." I recited the number, realizing his was the only one I remembered. All other numbers, including Katie's, were programmed into my phone. The girl dialed her cell, and I prayed Mike would answer a call from an unfamiliar number.

He did, thank God.

She began to explain, then stopped and asked me my name. I told her and she went back to the phone. "He wants to talk to you." She gave the phone to the kid and he passed it to me.

"Talia slipped me a mickey and dumped me at the old quarry. Everything is gone. Phone, gun, car. Please convince this fine young couple to give me a ride back to town."

"No wonder you didn't answer. I've been trying," Mike said. "Let me talk to the girl."

I handed the cell phone back in and she listened for a minute.

"Okay." She hung up. "We will take you."

The door unlocked, and I climbed in the backseat. "Thank you."

"The guy on the phone said you'll make it worth our while."

"Yes, definitely. Thank you, and again, I am sorry if I scared you."

"You did scare us. I fucking wet my pants," she said.

"You did?" Tim said. "This is my dad's car."

"Shut up and don't ever ask me out again."

I gave him McNally's address and he got the car turned around. I laid my head back, closed my eyes, and thanked God as my thoughts drifted to Lamar lying in the dirt.

44

The ride into town was silent for the most part. I learned the girl's name was Madison from the two phone calls she made, until I explained she shouldn't be telling friends about her experience because we didn't want the bad guys to learn her name. That stopped her. I had Tim park in the alley behind McNally's, where Mike was already waiting in his Jeep Wrangler. He climbed out when he spotted us.

"Wait here," I said. "I'll be right back."

"Dude, we need to go."

"No, I'll be back in a minute. My friend is not going to allow you to leave anyhow."

I jumped out of the car and hurried up the stairs to my condo, where I pulled on a pair of sneakers and a new T-shirt. I grabbed some money from my emergency cash in my nightstand.

Back in the alley, I handed the bills through the car window to Tim. "Two hundred."

"Whoa, thanks."

"Give her half. She earned it."

He counted out her share. "Thanks," she said.

"Here's another hundred to detail the car. Remember, do not talk about tonight and never go to the quarry again. Too dangerous."

"Don't worry about that," Tim said. "Thanks again."

They drove off and Mike walked over. "You okay?"

"Not sure. Head is still spinning, but we need to go. The deal is going down, or they wouldn't have tucked me away. I'm worried about Katie. Any word from Monica?"

"Nothing, but Katie has been calling all night because you did not respond."

"She okay? I guess my phone is at the bottom of the quarry. With my gun and car."

"Everything was jake the last time we talked."

"Call her, please. Find out if she talked to Monica."

"Here, you call." He handed me his cell. "I'll get you some water."

"Great idea, thanks." He went in McNally's through the kitchen door as I dialed.

She picked up on the first ring. "Mike, what's going on? Johnny is still not answering—"

"Slow down, it's me. I'm with Mike. All quiet there?"

"Yeah, just worried, scared. What happened?"

"Talia had other plans for me tonight. I'll explain later. Have you heard from Monica?"

"Yeah, she sent a text. Said she was on a case all day and was tired and headed home. That was a couple of hours ago."

No way Mad Dog Mattson would send a message saying she was tired. Plus, she said she was assigned to this case only.

"Johnny? You there?"

I paced around the alley. "Yeah. Did you tell her where you are?"

"Yes, she asked. I said I was here with Stan."

"Okay, sit tight. Keep the lights off, the doors locked, and the gun with you. Take off the safety. I don't have my phone, so call Mike with anything."

"You're scaring me."

"We are headed your way as soon as we can. Only talk to me or Mike. Do not text Monica. Do not respond to any of her messages. We'll stay in touch."

I closed the phone.

"She okay?" Mike asked, as he came with two bottles of water.

"So far." I gulped down the first one and the water revitalized me a bit. "I'm worried about Monica. We need to find her first, then head to the beach."

"Ideas?"

"No."

"All right, Detective. Start with what we know. Locations?"

"Talia's apartment, which is location unknown, the airfield, and the warehouse. Anthony DeRenzo's house. Katie has the address."

"Warehouse is closest."

"We'll need to break in."

Mike opened the garage door and grabbed some tools—a chisel, crowbar, hammer, a sledgehammer, a couple of flashlights—and threw them all in the back of his Jeep.

"I don't have a weapon," I said.

"Got you covered, partner. Let's go."

###

Two passes of the front of the one-story building that housed Entertainment Ventures showed no cars in the lot. We turned on the road that ran perpendicular to Commons Boulevard and drove past the left entrance to the rear of the building, then doubled back and parked. We cut the lights and sat for a few minutes in silence, hoping some activity would reveal itself. All quiet.

"Shall we." Mike handed me a 9mm Ruger.

I nodded. We got out of the Jeep. He took his 12-gauge shotgun, Beulah, from its mount on the roll bar, and we grabbed the tools from the back.

The rear parking area was also empty. No vehicles at Gary's Auto Body, and no activity at Amazing Graphics.

"Too quiet, partner."

"Hope this is not a waste of time," I said, "because I need to be at the beach with Katie and the unpredictable Stan."

"You see any cameras?"

"No. Not surprised if they are moving people in and out of here. Wouldn't want that on camera. Doubt an alarm, either."

"Let's go then."

We stayed next to the outer wall of the building as we made our way to the back door of Entertainment Ventures. The door was heavy steel.

"Only one way, brother," Mike said.

"Go for it. If they don't know we are here, they will in a second."

He handed me the shotgun and went to work, hammering the chisel between the door and the jamb, directly above the lock. He muscled it back and forth to create an opening large enough for the angled end of the crowbar. It took all two hundred and thirty of his Irish pounds, but on the third yank with the crowbar, the lock popped and the door swung opened. We both waited on the side of the door to avoid the gunfire, but nothing. All quiet.

We looked at each other, eyebrows up, not sure what to expect because we sure gave up the element of surprise.

He put a finger to his lips and took the first step into the cavernous warehouse. A moment later, he motioned for me.

We were both two steps into the darkness and stopped, listened. Silence. We clicked on the flashlights, then Mike held up a hand. "Wait, you hear that?" he whispered. "Listen."

We stood, motionless.

"Who's there? I need help." A soft raspy voice, from the opposite end of the warehouse, but recognizable.

We said it together: "Monica."

45

Inside the warehouse door was a living area with two sofas, a coffee table, and a television. Pizza boxes, fast-food wrappers, cups, and bags littered the table. The remnants of a recent meal. We aimed the flashlight beams farther into the space without regard to whomever could be waiting to mow us down. Three metal-framed beds lined the both walls, barracks style. Each bed had a small nightstand with a lamp, and carpeting covered the entire interior floor, so our footfalls were silent. After the third bed on the right were two racks of clothing, partitioning the room. On the other side of the clothes racks, our lights fell on another bed, this one with Monica strapped to it.

"Monica, it's us, Johnny and Mike."

She began to cry. "Oh, my God. How did…" Her voice was raspy, dry. "I'm sorry." She sobbed. "I never thought…"

"Don't talk," I said. "We're here, we got you."

Heavy twine lashed each ankle to the metal foot board and each arm to the sides of the bedframe. And she was naked. The stench of stale urine from soiled sheets hung in the air. Mike grabbed a blanket from one of the other beds and threw it over her. Adjacent to her bed was a kitchenette and beyond that a bathroom. I snapped on the kitchen light and found a knife in a drawer.

I cut her free. "Slowly, now...try to sit up."

"My knee." Her right knee was twice the size of her left.

We helped her into a sitting position on the side of the bed. Mike filled a glass with water, and we had her take sips.

"Your dream come true," she said, in a soft whisper. "Finally got to see me naked."

"Yes, but in my dream, it happens after a bottle of wine and dinner," I said.

"In mine, it happens in a cheap motel outside of town," Mike added.

"I love you guys." Her tears fell again. "Bathroom." She stood, pulled the blanket around her, balanced on her left leg and used my shoulder as a crutch and slowly hopped her way to the bathroom.

"Her clothes?"

He looked around and shrugged. The racks held every type of article of clothing for girls, plus the wall was lined with shelves full of shoes, purses, makeup, and cosmetics. Another unit had electronics, phones, tablets, and laptops. I picked out sweatpants and a T-shirt I thought would fit.

I knocked on the bathroom door. "You okay? I found some clothes." The door cracked opened and I handed them in.

"Give me a minute," she said. "Trying to get cleaned up."

"Take your time," I said, extremely happy we found her, but also eager to be with Katie at the cottage.

"You see this place?" Mike scanned the inside of the warehouse, now converted to a living quarters, with his flashlight. "They must house girls here while getting them adjusted." He shined the light on the wood paneled wall, which had a design of perforations in it. "Soundproofing. The holes in the panels deaden the sound. They could keep girls here for weeks and never be detected."

A *bang* on the steel door. We clicked off our flashlights and dropped to the floor. The bathroom door opened behind us and light spilled into the area as Monica hobbled out, moving slowly, massaging her wrists. "Some mad dog, huh...?" The darkness stopped her. "Guys?"

The light backlit her and made her an easy target. "Take cover." I said. I slid from my spot by the clothes rack and pulled her down beside me. We stayed motionless and silent for a full two minutes, until the door clanged again.

"Could be the wind," Mike said. "I'll go." He moved to the door in the dark and stepped outside, Beulah first. He ducked back in and did his best to secure the door closed with a now bent frame. "We should go."

I helped Monica up and plopped her on one of the beds while I took a pair of slip-on sneakers off the shelf for her. This place had Talia's mark all over it. The clothes all came from high-end department stores. No bargain-basement stuff for her.

"How long have you been here?"

"All day," she said. "Bill Davis called me this morning, said he had information, but only for me. Said he knew who I was and told me not to tell you. I was curious. I get to the airfield, and the next thing I know, my knee is whacked, and I am on the ground. Jumped from behind...some other guy who looks like Davis."

"His brother, Jacob."

"Then a rag over my mouth, ether maybe, and I go out. Woke up here tied to the bed. Not sure why they just didn't kill me."

Mike joined us. "They did—you would have been dead in two days."

"They wanted to humiliate me. Girls were here—four, I think, plus Talia and Dee Dee. They gave them food and clothes."

"Earlier tonight?"

"Yeah. They took turns taking a shower and as each one walked past me, she would stop and stare. I don't speak Spanish, but I think I was the example of what happens when you disobey. I can't believe you guys...I never thought anyone would find me...knee is killing me...I need something, juice. What time is it?"

"After two." Mike hustled off to the kitchen.

"They sent text messages to Katie from your phone. She is with Stan at my beach place. I wanted them out of sight tonight, but now I'm not so sure."

"We need to go," she said. "I have facial recognition on my phone as the password. What a mistake that was."

"You need a hospital, and we only have one vehicle."

She shook her head.

Mike got back with orange juice, which she gulped down, and two protein bars, and a bottle of pills. "Take some of these," he said, "for the swelling."

She swallowed a few. "Thanks. Let's go. We'll have time for my knee later." Neither Mike nor I moved, both of us deciding what we should do. "Now," she yelled.

He jumped up. "I'm going for my Jeep, it will be quicker than carrying you." He tucked his shotgun under his arm as he ran out.

"Where's your car?" she asked.

"You weren't the only one they wanted out of the way tonight."

She grabbed my hand. "At least we are still breathing."

46

"This is Detective Mattson. Roll a unit to the old quarry, report of a dead body. Right, Spring Hollow Road."

I explained to Mike and Monica how Lamar Shanks was Kenzie's dealer and accomplice in the blackmail attempt, and how I woke up next to him, only he was colder than the quarry water. I asked her to call it in. Even a drug dealer did not deserve to lie dead in the dirt.

She handed our only phone back to me. We lost two cars, two cell phones, and four guns, including Monica's three. We stayed in constant contact with Katie on our drive to Crescent Beach, via text. All was quiet, she reported.

"Slow down, Mike, coming up on your left," I said, as we turned on the access road for my property. The phone lit up, a message from Katie:

"I heard something. A car door."

"She heard a noise. I'm responding," I said.

"Stay quiet, we are almost there."

"Okay, Mike, fifty yards is my drive. Cut the lights."

He did, and we went at a slow crawl along the narrow road until we spotted Talia's Jaguar on the shoulder, near the entrance to my gravel driveway. My cottage was a hundred feet from the road and turning in would be louder than sounding an alarm.

"Talia is here," Monica said. "Surprise, surprise."

"Taking care of business herself." I hoped we were not far behind. Talia proved she had no room for loose ends. Kenzie and Lamar could be linked to her organization. Paul Ellison sniffed too close, as did Monica, who she left for dead. And my fate, she left to chance. I feared what waited for us at the end of the drive.

"Monica, move to the driver's seat. If the person driving that Jag comes up here and we don't, ram it if you need to," Mike said.

"Like hell! I'll be right behind you."

"You can't walk, and you don't have a weapon," I said. "Keep this." I handed her the phone. "Mike, ready?"

"Let's do it, brother."

He carried the twelve gauge and I had the Glock, and we walked single file on the edge of the driveway, staying off the noisy stone. The light from the moon was my friend earlier in the night at the quarry, but now we were illuminated with nowhere to hide. Low sand dunes were on either side, with no tall cover. Easy targets.

A blast broke the night silence. We both dropped to a crouch. Mike held up a hand and we listened. Nothing: no voices, no footsteps, nobody running for the road. My heart pounded. *Was that Katie taking a shot, or...?*

An engine started. Not a car, something smaller.

He turned to me. "You hear that?"

"It's my air compressor."

Then, *bam...bam...bam...bam...bam...bam!*

"Go," I said, and we stayed as low as possible until we got to the cottage. "Go around the back. I am going to the deck."

Bam, bam...bam...bam...bam...bam!

I hugged the side of the house as I moved closer to the front deck, which was on my left. The noise stopped; so did I. To listen.

The only sounds were the breeze off the ocean and the surf breaking on the beach. I waited as long as I could stand it, then peeked around the corner of the cottage.

There stood Katie, in the glow of the moonshine, the wind flicking her blonde hair, nail gun in her hand, the conquering soldier straddling her prey.

"Katie?" I said. "What...?" I stepped up as Mike came from the back. He followed me. On the deck was Anthony DeRenzo, out cold. She nailed his clothes to the boards, with him wearing them. She nailed around his body like a chalk outline. A handgun was beside him.

"Is he dead?" Mike said.

"No," she said, her breathing fast and heavy. Her adrenaline must be spiking at record levels. "I...I...took a shot..." Her eyes were wide and animated.

"Slow down," I said. "Tell us what happened."

"I heard a car door. So, I hid in the corner, but I could see him coming down the drive. I didn't want to be cornered in here if he came in, so I decided to wait outside to surprise him. He came up on the deck and I told him to stop. He didn't, and he came toward me, so I fired."

"You hit him?" Mike asked.

She shook her head. "Missed by a mile. Scared him, though, because he fell back—I guess tripped over himself, and hit his head on the rail. Then I got the nail gun."

Monica hobbled up on the deck, taking in the scene. "Holy shit. Are his clothes nailed to the..."

DeRenzo stirred, opened his eyes. "What the hell?" Tried to move his arms and legs. "Hey, let me up. What is this?"

Katie pressed the gun to his forehead. "Say one more word and I will put one in your brain."

"Whoa," Monica said. "Warrior Barbie, now who's the bad ass?"

47

"Where is Stan?" I took the nail gun out of her hand and led her away from a screaming Anthony DeRenzo.

"Hiding in the bedroom," Katie said.

We went inside and called for him.

He came out of the bedroom like a scared puppy, faced us, took in our collective gaze. "What happened? I heard shooting."

"Sit down," I said.

He sat on the sofa, and we helped Monica to my old leather recliner. I filled a plastic bag with ice for her knee, and Mike and I pulled in chairs from the kitchen. "Katie?" I motioned for her to sit.

She shook her head. In fact, she couldn't stop moving, fidgeting—still amped I'm sure.

DeRenzo's shouts drew Stan's attention. "Who's out there? Katie, did you shoot him?"

"Stan," I said, "you have three minutes to explain everything. No bullshit. Start talking."

He threw up his hands. "What do you mean? I already told you everything. Is that Anthony?"

"Detective Mattson is ready to arrest you, so I would stick to the truth if I were you."

"Arrest *me*? I'm a victim here. These people tried to blackmail me. Johnny, if not for you, I don't know what I would do."

"Stan, talk, now. We confirmed they flew girls in tonight; the FBI is on it. This is your one chance to come clean."

"The more you tell me now, the better it will be for you. Cooperate, and I help you cut a deal," Monica said.

"Deal? I was being blackmailed." He got up and paced around.

"Sit back down." I got up from my chair. He sat, and Mike and I stood in front of him. "We'll try this again, one more time."

He looked up at us with sad eyes.

"We confirmed it was your plane. Makes you an accessory, for starters. Then, add in the dead bodies. One police detective, Kenzie, and now Lamar Shanks."

"Who's he?"

"Kenzie's blackmail partner. Talia is adept at eliminating any ties to her business, so you can bet she will give you up in a second."

"You're talking like I need a lawyer or something." Stan sat back on the sofa, defiantly crossing his arms.

It was all Mike could handle. He stepped closer, bent down, and grabbed a fist full of his shirt, pulled him close and screamed in his face. "My partner, and this detective, were both left for dead tonight. Tell them what they need to know, now, or I take you out to the deck and put a nail into your wooden skull. Idiot." He pushed him into the sofa.

"Okay, okay." He ran a hand through his hair. "How about a drink?"

"No," I said.

We all had our arms crossed in front of us, waiting.

"Jesus, you should see yourselves. Scarier than the Steelers defensive line in the seventies."

Mike took a step forward. "Where are the girls now?"

He sat forward, elbows on knees and head in his hands, and stared at the floor as he talked. "On their way to New York. Dee Dee is driving them."

"What vehicle?"

"Anthony's. Probably."

"How long have you been involved in this?"

"Six months or so. I met Anthony first. Hired him as my pilot. We would talk about women while flying, as guys do. Me, anyhow. He tells me about this escort service, and eventually introduces me to Talia and Dee Dee, and I loved it. Much like what I told you, Johnny— it was easy. Girls to my loft and all. Then Talia approaches me about investing and it sounds fun. I transfer some money. Two weeks later, she hands me an envelope with ten grand in cash, said there is plenty more and explains her deal. I figure, no harm—she's taking care of these girls—so I go along.

"I agreed to finance all the plane trips and even bought a house outside Atlanta where they stay for a few nights to lay low in case they were followed. Then we fly them to the airfield at night." He looked at me. "You know about the warehouse?" I nodded. "They go there for a couple of days, and then Dee Dee drives them to New York. We are paid $15,000 per girl. $20,000 if they are underage."

"Kenzie?" I asked.

"She wanted in on the deal. She found out about the trafficking and wanted in. Talia and Dee Dee wanted nothing to do with her, so she got mad and cooked up the blackmail scheme to get me on her side. She was going to expose everything unless I talked Talia into bringing her into the business. Talia solved the problem. You were right—it was a message to me. But the message was to play by Talia's rules."

"How was I supposed to help?"

"I figured if I hired you, it would look legit that I was being blackmailed. I was scared at that point and couldn't see a way out."

"Where's Talia?"

"No idea."

"Stand up."

He did, and I threw the best right hook of my life, knocking him back over the sofa. Mike grabbed me before I dove over after him.

Stan pulled himself up. "You know what, John—I deserved that, didn't I?"

"Monica?" I said.

"With pleasure. Stan Shelton, you are under arrest for human trafficking and as many other charges as I can make stick. You have the right to remain silent, anything you say can and will be used against you in a court of law. You have the right to an attorney..."

I went outside to DeRenzo. "Where is Talia?"

A sick smile went across his face. "Everywhere."

I flicked on the air compressor, and picked up the nail gun and held it against his head. "Try again."

"How would I know? I'm sort of stuck here with you."

"Is she with Dee Dee?"

"You a cop?"

"You are not that lucky."

"Go to hell."

I fired a nail into the deck, a fraction of an inch from his ear. The sound itself probably did some damage. The door opened, and Katie and Mike ran out.

"All good here. Anthony was about to tell me where Talia is." I put the nail gun to the other side of his head. "Right?"

"I said, go to hell."

I fired again.

"All right. Jesus. Airfield. But you're too late."

"Yeah?" I hopped up. "Katie, I need your car keys."

I noticed the white, twin-engine plane on the tarmac as I pulled into the empty parking lot at the airfield. Was she still here? What exactly was I going to say: "Please don't leave, the FBI are on their way to arrest you"? Or was it to be, "Hey, I survived the quarry, here I am to take another beating"? Or, could I talk her into negotiating a plea deal, to use her words, "on the grounds she was actually helping these girls who would come here anyway?"

I was on a mission without a goal. A fool's mission.

I hopped out of Katie's Honda and clicked off the safety on the Glock. The place was deserted, or so I thought.

"We're ready to go." A man's voice, somewhere near the hangar.

Bobby Rodriguez? I stayed against the outside wall of the terminal. Maybe I was not too late after all. I stopped at the corner of the building; any farther and I would be exposed.

From behind me: "Delarosa."

I spun around, and in the fraction of a second it took for my brain to register the Davis brothers, I caught a movement out of my left eye. A bash to my head and a sharp pain, and I was on the ground. The weight of two bodies on me, pinning me down. My arms yanked behind my back and my hands tied together. My ankles bound and trussed to my hands. Hogtied.

Brothers Davis pulled me up by my armpits and dragged me to the tarmac, with my knees scraping the asphalt and blood trickling off my forehead, into my left eye.

She approached. They held me up, and I raised my face as high as I could.

"Never thought I'd see you here. I am genuinely happy you are alive." She bent over so we were more eye to emerald eye. "Nasty cut. Might scar."

"Talia. Don't do this."

"What—leave you to die, or flee the country?"

"It's over." I couldn't hold my head up against the pain from the wound, the blood dripping.

She gently lifted my chin. "All these years, can you believe our paths crossed again? I am thrilled we had a chance to visit." The engines started on the Beechcraft. "My ride. Until we meet again. Could be in this world, maybe some other." She reached behind her with her other hand and flashed my Beretta in front of me. "A souvenir of our time together."

She let my chin drop, but I did my best to crane my head up as she walked to the plane.

She stopped, turned around, and came back a few paces toward us. "I really am glad you are alive." She fired two bullets, one into each Davis.

They fell back, taking me with them.

The twin engines roared as I struggled against the ties around my wrists, but all I could do was shimmy and maneuver my body around to watch as the plane rolled along the runway, climb into the air, and faded into the morning sky.

48

Katie set a drink in front of each of us.

"Hey, there's fruit floating in my drink," Mike quipped.

"Try it," she said. "My new concoction. Similar to a Manhattan."

Me, Mike, and Monica were lined up at the bar in McNally's while Katie served. Monica balanced herself on a stool with a wrapped knee and crutches. We all sipped. "Hey, not bad," I said. "What's in it?"

"Bulleit bourbon, sweet vermouth, orange bitters, cherries, and a slice of orange. I call it... ready?...the Delarosa."

"What?" I said.

"I'll drink to that." Monica sipped. "Delicious."

"A tribute to my favorite private investigator and my boss. The one who promised to take me shooting."

We all raised a glass. "A little fancy," I said, "but tasty."

"There is still fruit in my drink," Mike said.

"Funny, funny," Katie said. "Goes on the menu today."

"And I will take you shooting. Not sure if we should go to the range, or to the lumber yard and buy a two-b- four," I said.

"Speaking of which." Mike reached under the bar and pulled a picture from an envelope. "Proof of the greatest capture in law enforcement history." He held up an 8x10 photo of Anthony DeRenzo nailed to the deck. Written with marker in the bottom margin was "Warrior Barbie always gets her man."

"You took a picture?" Katie asked.

"Damn right. No way I could pass it up." He stuck the picture in the wooden frame around the mirror behind the bar. "Saved for prosperity. And some wild stories."

"I love it!" She danced around, hands thrust in the air. "Now who needs their license?"

"Whoa, save the party for later. We got company," Mike said, as we followed his gaze to the front window. Captain Elliott Lane was out of his black sedan and on his way in.

"Captain. Welcome to McNally's," I said.

"I'm glad you are all here. Wanted to update you on the case. First, Mattson, how is the knee?"

"Bad bruise. Should be back on the job in two weeks."

He nodded. "Happy it's not worse. More good news— we found your Camaro in a barn on Jacob Davis's farm. Not a scratch on it."

"They knew not to mess with me."

"Delarosa," he said. "Bad news. Your car is at the bottom of the quarry. Sorry, but a decision will be made on whether it is worth pulling out. Hope you have decent insurance."

"I do, but not sure it covers car drowned by criminals."

They all laughed.

"I'll try to make a case for you. No promises."

"Fair enough."

"The NYPD picked up Daniella DeRenzo as she approached the Holland Tunnel, leaving the city. All because of your efforts, though. Can't thank you enough. No sign of Talia Thorne. The FAA is reviewing all radar from the other night. Can't find Bobby Rodriguez either, so we assumed he was her pilot."

"What about the girls she brought in?" I asked.

"No luck yet, and DeRenzo is not talking."

"And Stan?"

"Bawling like a baby. He'll plead out. His lawyer is spinning him as a victim in an elaborate scam."

"Not surprised," I said.

Captain Lane turned his attention to my tall, blonde bartender. "Are you Katie Pitts?"

"Yes."

"I heard about what you did." He reached across the bar and shook her hand, then gave her a business card. "We could use strong, fearless women like you on the PCPD. Give me a call."

"Thank you. I just might do that."

Handshakes all around and Lane turned to leave but stopped. "Oh, Mike. Abby says hello. We'd love to have you over for dinner some night. Been a long time."

If I ever wanted to capture a moment in time, it was then. The big red Irishman went so pale, his freckles disappeared. "Sure, I'd love to, but...I thought...you two..." He stumbled all over his words.

"Split up? Yeah, vicious rumor. I caught her having an affair. Mike Curtis from the Fourth Precinct? Transferred him to Traffic, packed my stuff, and moved out. Lasted three days—she apologized, and I moved back. We talked it over, realized we are meant for each other, and now everything is better than ever."

"Oh. Glad to hear." Mike had a nonplussed expression across his face.

"I'll give you a call."

Captain Lane went out, and Mike stared at the floor. He dared not even look at us, especially Katie. "Do not even say a word," he said.

"Are. You. Kidding. Me," she said, each word slow and deliberate. "They were together the whole time you were...I was so right. Damn. The definition of friends with benefits. You and Curtis took turns in Captain Lane's bed. Every time he was out, you were...two of you...oh my God. A traffic jam on Abby Road."

Mike's entire body turned red and the moment was more than funny. I poured him a quick shot of Irish whiskey and he threw it back.

She climbed on top of the bar. "Ladies and gentlemen, I am the queen of relationships."

"Okay, you were right. So?"

She hopped down. "So, now you know to consult me with all relationship issues."

"Wait," Monica said. "I definitely missed something."

The door opened and the mail carrier came in with letters and a small box addressed to me.

Katie offered me a knife. "Are you going to open it?"

"Nah, I will take it upstairs."

"Now that we are done with my humiliation, I have a question." Mike looked at me. "Why do you think she spared you? Talia killed everyone who got close except you."

I contemplated telling them how I pulled a skinny, malnourished, abused teen from an ungodly vile situation, but it would only lead to more questions. "A story for another day."

Monica's new phone buzzed. "My ride is here." She hopped off the barstool and balanced herself with the crutches. "Hey, you earned a hug," she said to me.

Mike and Katie came around the bar for hugs, too.

I opened my arms, but instead, she pulled my face to hers and planted a full, open-mouth kiss on me. She broke away. "Always wanted to do that." She then grabbed Katie and kissed her full on the mouth. "That too." She whispered something into Katie's ear, who was so stunned she froze in place. To me: "I should retire and come work here."

"After that kiss, you can work here anytime."

She tossed us a wave as she hobbled out. "Later, friends."

Katie couldn't move.

"Are you okay?" I asked.

She nodded and slowly walked, as if she were in a trance, to the kitchen.

I looked at Mike. "Don't see that every day."

"Not complaining."

Upstairs in my condo, I poured two fingers of bourbon into a rocks glass and pulled Charlie Parker's *One Night in Birdland* from my shelf and slid it into the CD player. I needed some cool sax after the past few days.

The box did not have a return address, but somehow, I knew the contents. I sliced the tape and slowly opened it.

A note on top:

Johnny, until we meet again.

Love,

Talia

"No doubt we will, Talia. No doubt we will."

I took the pink bunny from the box. Never did I think the young girl I rescued a long time ago would come back into my life. I took the bunny, the note, and my drink to my balcony and stretched out on my chair.

There are people who travel through your life who are insignificant, and then there are those who leave an indelible impression. Talia Thorne's lifelong impact on me was full of conflicting emotions. My heart broke when I found her in the squalor of the Hotel Atlantic, and I violated so many rules and regulations the department could have fired me three times.

I was more than grateful to discover she was alive, and successful, and thriving, only to be disappointed by her chosen and twisted lifestyle. And my heart was touched to learn she still held a spot for me in her heart. The damage she suffered as a child influenced and controlled her behavior. There was no excuse for her criminality, but for me, and maybe only me, it was understandable.

I took my time finishing my bourbon, staring out at the city. Wondering. What was her name? Did she even know her real name? Where did she go? Stan's money landed in a bank in the Cayman Islands. Would the island be her first stop, or was the bank only a transfer account, with the funds instantly moved elsewhere? She could be anywhere on this globe by now. A beach, a mountain. Or she could be right here in Port City. Short hair, different color, a new name, a new identity. Would I recognize her? Certainly.

I placed the pink bunny, the note, and her note from twenty years ago, in the box and tucked it away on the top shelf of my bedroom closet.

"Until we meet again."

49

The limousine door opened, and we slid out. I caught two of the valet guys sneaking a second glance at her, and who could blame them. A hostess opened the door; we walked in, her arm in mine.

"Johnny Delarosa. Good evening and welcome."

"Hello, Charles."

"I have the perfect table waiting for you. Follow me."

She whispered to me. "You know the maître de?"

"I get around."

She wore a tight royal-blue dress that stopped three inches above her knee, a plunge of a neckline, but not too low, accented with a sapphire and diamond necklace. Her matching slingback heels accentuated her long, shapely legs and her trademark blonde hair fell in waves to the middle of her back. The Blue Coral Lounge was perfectly packed, and Charles led us through a maze of tables to ours at the front of the room. She turned every head in the place. Male and female. It was a Bond girl, show-stopping scene if there ever was one.

"You certainly know how to make an entrance."

She smiled. "Thank you."

A waiter appeared. "Two dry martinis up, with your best gin, and olives," I said.

"Yessir."

"Martinis? Fancy," Katie said.

"Top shelf tonight." A jazz quartet was on stage, putting a new spin on "Dream A Little Dream of Me." The band had a female singer named Seely, and she had a soulful, sultry voice that did a cool justice to the Ella tune.

"Even though we maintain our employer-employee relationship, I want to say you are absolutely stunning tonight."

"Why, thank you, Mister Delarosa. I appreciate everything you did. I can't believe we are at the Blue Coral."

"You deserve a night on the town. I'm surprised you are not wearing all black."

"Aren't you funny. I think my Monica phase is over."

"What did she say to you the other day, after she planted the kiss?"

"She said she will teach me to use my sexuality not to attract men, but to control them."

"And?"

"Mons is unique, intense, fun, and I can learn from her, but I think I am better off being myself. All that macho stuff is not me. I need to learn to use my own skills and to discover and develop my own talents."

"Truer words were never spoken. I'm impressed." I remembered the night I pulled her from a warehouse and how she came back asking for a job. Mike and I were so amused we couldn't refuse. She had since transformed our lives and I couldn't imagine the bar and my work without her. She was the closest I would ever come to having a daughter, and the pride welled in me.

"Are you the same woman who nail gunned a man to a deck? I heard about you."

"Don't be ridiculous. A woman of my grace, class, and sophistication wouldn't dream of touching a hammer, let alone some filthy nail gun."

"My mistake."

The martinis arrived and we toasted. "To your future as a private detective," I said.

"And to my friend, employer, mentor, and the man who has saved me from myself more times than I can count." She raised her glass, then sipped. "Whoa, strong."

"Hey, every Bond girl can drink a martini."

"I'll take it slow. Don't want to ruin the perfect evening."

The singer, Seely, called for everyone's attention. "Down front here is my good friend, Johnny." She waved and I waved back. "And this next song goes out to the beautiful blonde at his table. Katie, this is for you."

The band eased its way into "The Way You Look Tonight."

"You know her, too?" she asked.

"I get around."

The music flowed over us and I couldn't help but to sit back and take in the wonder of Katie. So grateful this beautiful, smart, funny, quirky person filled my life.

A smile on her face and a tear in her eye, she reached across the table and put her hand on mine.

ACKNOWLEDGEMENTS

Publishing a book is a team effort and I have a great team! Brandi Doane McCann once again did a wonderful job designing the cover for the book. Much thanks!

My editor, Faith Williams, always works overtime cleaning and polishing what I have written. I am grateful for her expert guidance. A big thank you to my proofreading team: Helene, Cassidy, Mark, and Matt, who spent a lot of time finding errors and making corrections!

A special debt of gratitude to Corbin and Larry Nulton, of Nulton Aviation, Johnstown, PA, for their consultation on the technical aspects of "flying under the radar." The father and son team are experienced pilots, businessmen, and more importantly, trusted friends. They do own a twin-engine Beechcraft, but I assure you it is used only for good, and not for evil. Thanks guys!

Thank you to my brother Matt, for his expertise on the weaponry described in the book, and to my brother Mark, for his constant support and promotion of the series.

A heartfelt thank you to my wife, Helene, for her constant love, support, and encouragement. And a thank you to my writing partners, Lucy and Kent, who keep us all young.

This book is dedicated to three smart, funny, hard-working, and extraordinary individuals. My children: Brian, Kevin, and Cassidy. Thank you for your love, inspiration, and support. You make me proud every day. I love you.

Johnny Delarosa will return!
For more information,
please visit:

www.davidstever.com

Be sure to join the
mailing list for news,
reviews, and updates!

Thank you!